ALEX DRAKE
and
FRIENDS

ALEX DRAKE
and
FRIENDS
Wasor Island

AADITYA RAJ

Published by
Rupa Publications India Pvt. Ltd 2021
7/16, Ansari Road, Daryaganj
New Delhi 110002

Sales centres:
Allahabad Bengaluru Chennai
Hyderabad Jaipur Kathmandu
Kolkata Mumbai

Copyright © Aaditya Raj 2021

This is a work of fiction. Names, characters, places and incidents are either the product of the author's imagination or are used fictitiously and any resemblance to any actual person, living or dead, events or locales is entirely coincidental.

All rights reserved.
No part of this publication may be reproduced, transmitted, or stored in a retrieval system, in any form or by any means, electronic, mechanical, photocopying, recording or otherwise, without the prior permission of the publisher.

ISBN: 978-93-90356-59-1

First impression 2021

10 9 8 7 6 5 4 3 2 1

The moral right of the author has been asserted.

Printed at Thomson Press India Ltd, Faridabad

This book is sold subject to the condition that it shall not, by way of trade or otherwise, be lent, resold, hired out, or otherwise circulated, without the publisher's prior consent, in any form of binding or cover other than that in which it is published.

To mom and dad,
who're always fond of adventure

Contents

Intro: A few words from the author... / ix

1. The Journey Begins / 1
2. The Journey's Interrupted / 9
3. The Weird Island / 17
4. The Rough Rescue Plan and the First Day on the Island / 29
5. The Traces of the Mystery / 45
6. The Terrific Mystery / 52
7. The First Two Tasks / 72
8. The Helpful Dream and 'Beauties First!' / 83
9. Life's Gloomy / 98
10. The 'Almost Dead' Experience / 111
11. DarkService / 121
12. Technical Madness / 131
13. Death Is Mandatory / 139
14. The Dumpster of the Dead / 162
15. Let's Wriggle Out! / 188
16. Reunion / 221

INTRO

A few words from the author...

Dear reader, you're going to read something incredible. It's a story of three close friends, who set off on a journey to relax and enjoy their time. But fate had other plans for them...

The epicentre of this tale revolves around the friendship among Angelina, Lester and Alex, and is set in the year 2010.

Angelina is the daughter of Clinton and Susan Barrette. At the age of eighteen, she recently completed her schooling. She has a beautiful face; her pea-green eyes are extremely charming. She is slim and has thick, wavy brown hair, falling a little below her shoulders. She dresses up pretty well, usually rocking T-shirt and jeans. Quite childlike at times, Angelina is generous and intelligent within.

Lester is the son of Isabella and Eric Watson, who runs an electronic shop in Florida. He is tall, slightly fat, with long spiky hair and a large crooked nose. He had recently celebrated his 20th birthday. His voice is considered a little *too* loud. He is an electronics' master. He is always jovial and carefree. Sometimes, he even wears T-shirts with imprints such as, 'Go on. Let's see what you can ruin :}.' So is his attitude towards life's bumps. Alex is his best friend. But, 'Who is Alex?' you want to ask? Then...I guess I'll need to tell you about our protagonist.

Alex Drake is the son of one of the biggest business entrepreneurs in United States, Clive Drake. His mother is Lucy Drake, who owns a chain of hotels in the country. In a family of millionaires, Alex manages a part of his father's huge business. At age 22, he is older than Lester and Angelina, and so is his experience in life.

He had pitched in a part of his father's business and is now a renowned shale oil & gas merchant. A patient man, he has deep-set eyes, and short, dark brown hair. He is considered to be knowledgeable and *brainy*. At least *that's* what his friends call him, as

A few words from the author...

Alex had helped many of them get through difficult situations when they were teenagers.

The three childhood pals live in Florida. They somehow reach at an unpredictably weird place and come across unprecedented experiences. They uphold their sense of humour and stay courageous during adverse times, and thereby fight together to overcome the hurdles.

Start reading... Soon you'll get the hang of this tale.

Chapter 1

The Journey Begins

Alex had just been woken up by the shrill sound of the alarm clock. Lazily, he made an effort to get up from the bed. When he peeped through the window, he noticed Lester hurrying towards his house. In no time, Alex heard the doorbell ring.

Alex rushed down to the living room on the ground floor to receive Lester. As soon as he opened the door, Lester said, 'Man, I've got some incredible news for you.'

'What incredible news, dude?'

'Guess what...?' he said, with a broad smile on his face. 'I've won something.'

'That's great. But *what*...?'

'I have won a contest. Can you imagine the reward...? I bet you can't. It's nothing out of the ordinary though, but for me... it's priceless.'

'Now just let the cat out of the bag, Lester,' Alex replied, casually giving a *I see you're hyperactive and excited but I don't see what the fuss is about so tell me quickly* look.

'I have won a two-way trip to Japan. Isn't it thrilling?' continued Lester happily, without giving time to Alex to say anything.

'What's more exhilarating is that I have won three tickets for the journey. I have an option to go either with my parents or with any two people of my choice,' Lester said.

'Maybe he *is* really enthusiastic,' Alex wondered.

'Nice job. You've won a contest. Lemme guess... Don't seem to get it... What's it about?'

'You know, I'm good at maths, it was National Maths Quiz... and that's what has earned me three tickets. Travelling out of the city... well, to me, *that's* just incredible. And now, here lies the real surprise for you. I've booked three tickets to Japan.'

Pausing in between, he continued 'And you know... without asking you beforehand, I've booked the tickets.'

The Journey Begins

'I *am* surprised. But what's so incredible in getting out of the country? I have travelled to foreign lands several times.'

Alex soon realized his mistake in saying that, and recalled that Lester hadn't even travelled out of the state before, and that's why he was so excited.

Quickly acting, trying to distract Lester from the *incredible* topic, Alex questioned why Lester was especially telling him that he'd booked the tickets.

'I want you and Angelina to accompany me to Japan. This is the first time we're getting a chance to go somewhere really far away together, plus, I've already got the tickets ready... And, and... I don't wanna miss this opportunity,' he said.

Alex thought about it for a moment.

'I'm sorry buddy, but...I guess I can't go as my ships have left for business and haven't returned yet.' Alex felt it hard to refuse Lester's *once-in-a-lifetime with friends* opportunity, but he had to do so. He couldn't leave his business work unsupported. Especially at a time when other companies were aspiring to compete and snatch his monopoly in the market, he couldn't rely on anyone, except his manager, who was away on a business tour.

Lester plopped himself on the couch, apparently disappointed. It seemed as if he was mad at himself for not asking Alex whether he was available for the trip. 'Sup?' Lester said.

'Sorry, but never mind. Just chill, man. We'll get another trip planned. And I promise, it will be soon. Help yourself to some sandwiches. I have a little urgent work pending, and I'll be back here in a few minutes,' said Alex as he gestured towards some packaged cucumber sandwiches kept on the living room table and went upstairs to his room, leaving Lester downright there, apparently lonely and hopeless. While Alex was getting upon his investments' account calculations, his cell phone rang and he spoke to someone for a while. His general manager, who was supposed to return the next week, was fatefully set to return earlier due to the postponement of a business conference. He would manage everything; he'd assured Alex during the call.

Alex was relieved and delighted. He could now join Lester and Angelina for the trip. 'A trip with my best friends, whoa!' Alex couldn't believe his luck.

He quickly ran downstairs and told Lester that his manager is going to return earlier than scheduled, which meant that he could join them.

The Journey Begins

Lester was overjoyed, his gloomy face at once cheering up with this unexpected news. Then, they decided to head to Angelina's residence and tell her about the plan.

When Angelina opened the door, Lester immediately told her about their plan of going to Japan with her.

'Well, I would've loved to come with you guys, but the thing is... See, I am down with high fever and my parents are away. I haven't told them about it yet as I didn't want to disturb them unnecessarily. They'll be returning soon, probably within 2-3 days. Till then I'm taking adequate doses of the medicines,' she replied. *She didn't say prescribed by the doctor*, Alex noted.

Angelina confessed. 'Truly speaking, I am on self-medication. I'm using the medicines left in the store, and managing somehow until my parents return.'

Alex felt sorry for her 'Okay. But let's head for the doctor's, like, *right now*. C'mon, we'll take you there.'

'No, Alex, I understand you're trying to help me, but I can't come along. I'm short of money, and thus reluctant to consult a doctor. Mum and dad will return soon to aid me. Until then...' Angelina reasoned, as her voice faltered suddenly.

Alex offered to spend for her, which she could pay back later. She agreed reluctantly. 'Let's get going, then.'

At the doctor's clinic, while examining Angelina carefully, he told them that there was nothing to worry about, and Angelina just had a seasonal flu. She would need to take some medicines for two to three days. The doctor then gave her a list of medicines and accepted the fee from Alex. After leaving the clinic, they bought the prescribed medicines from a nearby drugstore.

Subsequently, they went to their respective houses and started packing for the tour, which was four days hence.

A day before leaving, Lester and Alex went to Angelina's house to ascertain whether she was well enough for the trip.

'I guess I'm fine now,' she replied, and turned towards Alex, 'Thanks to you. Otherwise... this trip with you guys wouldn't have been possible.'

'You're most welcome. We'll get going now. And, by the way, thanks for the reassurance.'

The next day, Lester and Alex picked up Angelina from her residence in Alex's chauffeur-driven BMW-3

Series. They reached the airport in about 20 minutes, and the chauffeur drove back to Drake residence after dropping them. Angelina had showed up with a lot of luggage. She had brought two suitcases and a big bag besides her handbag. Lester and Alex had to help her carry some of her baggage. As they entered the airport, Angelina moved ahead of them, singing under her breath.

'Isn't this a lot of stuff? It's heavy, too. What does she carry with her in these? We just manage with just one suitcase. What's in these... stones?' Lester whispered to Alex.

'You know what, I think she has brought a big monster in it. Gosh... this bag is so big. What stuff does she bring? I suggest we drop it. Then the whole airport will see Angelina's tantrums,' said Alex.

'That's an awesome idea. What a sight would it be...! But, I guess we better *not* try to act accordingly. Otherwise... you know how she could react and make us miserable in public,' Lester smiled.

After the boarding passes were issued and luggage check-in done, they went through the mandatory security check. It was noon, and there was another one and a half hour left for the airplane to take-off. They sat in the waiting area, which was right in front of their boarding gate—gate number 4—Alex's unlucky number.

Throwing away the numerology-related lucky-unlucky ideas, Alex got himself busy with attending calls. He had to schedule business meetings with a few European companies, which he was now postponing for fifteen days. Lester was enjoying the snacks fetched from the vending machine, while Angelina dozed off in her seat.

After about 45 minutes, the boarding gate opened and passengers started making their way towards the aircraft. The three friends boarded the business class in about 15 minutes. After everyone had settled down, the plane took off, soaring through the clouds within seconds.

Chapter 2

The Journey's Interrupted

While the plane was taking off, Lester shut his eyes. He had never travelled by air until that moment. Moreover, he was acrophobic. Alex had thoroughly enjoyed the take-off, looking down the view through the window. Angelina, sitting next to him, was drowsy again due to the effect of medication.

After reaching the desired flight level, the plane turned towards Japan and levelled at height. The seat belt signal was taken off.

Relieved at last, Lester tugged Alex at the arm and said, 'Man, wasn't that frightening?'

'You are a bigger scaredy cat than I thought. Just relax! There's no need to freak out,' Alex replied, amused. His words helped bring Lester to normalcy.

Angelina woke up as the plane suddenly experienced turbulent weather and started shaking vigorously. She grew pale with unforeseen apprehensions.

In no time the pilot announced, 'Due to heavy turbulence and technical issues the aeroplane has suffered damage, and has to make an emergency water landing. We are sorry for the inconvenience caused. Please stay alert and help others.' He further added, 'But please ensure that you aid *yourself* first before assisting others.'

The trio and most of the people in the plane just froze in their seats, fear spreading on each passenger's face.

Alex couldn't believe it at first. He thought, 'I have travelled a lot and have never experienced anything like this before. How could this happen at this very moment?' A chill ran down his spine as here remembered the boarding gate at the airport—Gate No. 4. 'My intuition wasn't wrong. It's indeed my unlucky number. This time, too. And almost each time I got hurt before, it was always the fourth of the month. Whenever I have lost something valuable, it was related to the number 4. I never believed in all this. But now, whether coincidentally or otherwise, it seems as if we're in grave danger,' a shocked Alex thought as he reflected over his past.

Lester chided Alex with bulging eyes, giving him a *I told you so* look and said, '*That's* why I am a scaredy cat.'

Angelina went out cold. They splashed some water on her face. In a while, she gained consciousness and stammered, 'What the–? Have we reached Tokyo?'

Before Alex was able to ascertain this sudden change in surroundings, the plane had landed on the shallow part of an ocean. Without assurance of survival, each passenger and crew member tried to save his life. People scurried to leave the aircraft and jumped into the ocean. They were pushed around by the strong current, and eventually they surrendered themselves to wherever the flow took them, with each being oblivious of the plight of their fellow passengers. Likewise, the trio too put their life vests on, and sadly and unwillingly dived into the icy-cold ocean.

They had carried their handbags along with them. Luckily, they didn't lose their money as they had kept it in their waterproof wallets. This gave Alex a sense of momentary relief. But he was extremely morose for losing his checked-in luggage, including his valuable laptop that contained the list of his digital trading contracts. But he had not lost hope yet.

When the plane eventually sank, fortunately it was near an island. Pointing towards it, he told his fellow comrades to follow him there. He had no idea whether any of the other passengers also tried to reach the island. Moreover, he couldn't spot any buildings on the island, which meant it was uninhabited and there was a fair chance of encountering wild animals. But they had no other choice.

Fortunately, Alex knew how to swim, thanks to a really embarrassing moment in the past.

'I must not let my mind wander into a series of humiliating experiences,' Alex thought.

While moving through the water, Alex recalled his school days, when he always wanted to know how the underwater world looked like. He was mesmerized by the seas and oceans about which he had read in his school textbooks. But the current situation did not allow him to explore life underwater. He had to safeguard himself and his friends first.

However, out of curiosity he couldn't resist diving underwater and taking a quick look into the vast ocean. He spotted a variety of aquatic animals and delightfully colourful fishes, but this was not what he had hoped to see. He had wanted to have a glimpse of the beautiful and incredible world of flora and fauna, which he had read about while at school. Soon, he realized the water was shallow and laughed at himself. *That* amazing world could only be spotted in deep water. Unaware of the forthcoming danger, he went on swimming towards the island. All of sudden he heard a noise. It was from a fellow passenger. 'Wha—why did that woman behind me scream? Wait... What did she say? Kill what? Eh? A killer whale!' he realized. 'More trouble. Let's get out of this danger zone.'

Unfortunately, when he spotted it, he felt as if the deadly creature had made eye contact with him, and had started heading towards him and his friends. He quickly shouted and informed his friends, who were not very far from him.

After Lester and Angelina realized that they were being pursued, they panicked and started praying, 'Oh, Jesus! Save us!'

Alex moved closer to them and asked them to stay strong. 'This is not the time to fear the whale. We need to act quickly and get AWAY from that being to reach safely on to the island,' he shouted at the top of his voice.

'The only way of escaping is to swim as fast as possible and reach the island. So let's do this without wasting any more time,' continued Alex.

Alex swam as quickly as he could, while his friends followed him. As they got closer to the island, Alex still felt the looming danger of the deadly creature, as if it were still following them. Alex and Lester safely reached the island but Angelina was breathless. Once she reached the island, she fainted. While the boys were helping her, they noticed that the killer whale had drifted off to another path and pounced at some of the fellow passengers, making them its prey.

'That's why we were getting so scared, and prayed for our safety,' Lester reasoned. 'I can't believe we're still alive,' he sighed.

'And together, too,' added Alex.

'Holy cow... The whale is out of sight now. Seems like we are safe,' said Angelina joyfully, her face still showing a hint of drowsiness. She had miraculously regained consciousness.

Finally, after having escaped from the clutches of the killer whale, the three of them started exploring the island. It appeared strange at first. The trees on it were not straight, but bent at acute angles. Moving further, they found huge and unfamiliar paw marks of a creature on the soil, with each paw comprising eight to ten long, broad fingers. The trio looked at each other, expressions of fear and anxiety writ large on their faces.

Moreover, the grass didn't appear to be fresh; the acidic grass was slightly bent, reflecting paw marks on the wet soil, which indicated that heavy animals had trampled upon the grass. The ground was uneven too, as if hundreds of meteors had crashed there. The island reeked of a foul smell, which emanates from a large group of people who had not bathed for a whole year. Then there was the smell of urine, faeces and dead animals. There were no signs of any human habitation.

'Ho-hum. I need to confess something. I have always wished to be on an island like this. I love to watch the beautiful and majestic aquatic world, which thrills me. But, I'm sorry for daydreaming on such a dangerous moment. This... this *negligence* of mine could've cost us our lives. Thanks to the lady passenger, whose shrill voice distracted and alarmed me and I saw that killer whale in the nick of the time,' reasoned Alex.

'Okay, you're forgiven,' said Lester in a bossy tone.

Alex and Angelina laughed at his silly joke of acting like the headmaster of *Alex is the only student* school.

But the island's weirdness bothered Alex. It added to his perception that this place was dangerous and they needed to struggle hard to survive in this unknown and dangerous island.

\..\... `'

Chapter 3

The Weird Island

Lester said to Alex, 'Bro, isn't this looking weird?'

'Well, I think that this place isn't weird. It is *extraweird*. I know that's a wrong prefix I'm adding there, but, you know, I just feel like it. Kinda gross.'

'It's dangerous, too,' Angelina added.

'I agree, but we have no other choice,' said Lester, shaking his head. 'All I can say is that we have to keep ourselves safe on this island to survive.'

As the three were conversing, all of a sudden Alex heard strange sounds. Apart from Lester's jokes, his attention drifted towards the noises, which resembled a mix of whinnying and roaring voices.

'It seems like we're not alone here,' said Alex in a low voice, sensing that they were being stalked.

Lester and Angelina shuddered, and reported hearing the same sounds.

'Maybe we should hide somewhere and let the animal, or whatever it is lose track and go away,' suggested Angelina.

All of them agreed unarguably and this remedy passed to the next level of execution without any examination or result. Later, on Alex's instructions, they set out to find a safe place on the islet.

They moved on, searching for a secure hideaway, but it was a difficult task. After looking around for about an hour, they found a dark cavern. Lester said, 'This place looks safe enough to me for now. Let's get in. Hopefully we'll spend the night here.'

'Like...cavemen?' Alex asked.

'Well, narrowing the possibilities to the tiniest bit of problems, I think...yes.'

But Angelina showed signs of nervousness.

'I can't risk my life. I mean, I do not agree because there can be another wild animal waiting for us in there to eat us alive. What if that turns out to be true? I guess all dangerous animals live in caves,' she said.

'Don't worry, Angelina. We'll guard you if any of your "imaginations" try to play hide and seek with you,' said Alex, laughing.

Angelina looked frustrated but pocketed the insult without saying anything.

No living creature was in sight when they reached near the entrance of the cave. They were just about to get inside when something stopped them. But the animal wouldn't budge. It had come searching for them near the area around the cave. That's when Alex saw the deadly creature.

He couldn't believe his eyes. 'This is beyond my imagination. It can't be real,' thought Alex.

All of them were startled at its gaze. It was an unusual animal, never seen or heard about before.

It was as big as an elephant, with a horn sprouting like a rhino. The skin was dusty, rough and brown, as if it always lived in a sandstorm-prone place. A four-legged animal, with eight to ten fingered paws, face as if it were... There can be no more resemblances. It was so peculiar.

It looked quite menacing, and more so because of its hyperactive attitude. Though it was too big to move swiftly, yet it was running all around furiously.

'I think it is gonna kill us—brutally,' said Lester.

Witnessing the strangeness of that animal, Alex whispered to Lester, 'Man, now I am really sure that this is the weirdest island I have ever seen.'

'But really, do you think that this isn't scary? I feel like it *is*.'

'Hey, Lester. Just keep calm. We'll soon be through this. We'll definitely find some way out. There's no need to be scared.'

'Yup.'

To make the atmosphere a little lighter, they started to think of a name for the animal. After a while, they all agreed on the name honoereon, as it bore a horn and looked similar to a rhino.

They decided to wait behind an overgrown bush to let the honoereon go away on its own. Their plan eventually succeeded, as the animal turned away and took a different path.

But there was no time to rejoice. Soon, they came to know that there was another wild animal in the cave. It made a feeble, hushed sound. Fortunately, Alex heard it in time. He suspected that it might pounce stealthily and gulp them down. He then whispered and told his friends about the presence of the beast in the cave. Angelina went pale and looked extremely frightened.

She had warned him earlier about her gut feeling regarding something dangerous residing inside the cave, but Alex had not bothered to listen, and instead pulled her leg. Alex was enraged for landing himself and his friends into such a situation. He lamented his ill-luck.

'This is not the time to argue and get mad at someone, especially me. We need to act fast,' he quietly told her.

'Is there a place here that has a large bulletin board marked as SAFE?' asked Lester, apparently trying to make things light.

Alex suggested that they quietly move away from the cave when the animal wasn't looking or paying attention. But, as they started to escape, the animal suddenly turned around. It earlier had its back towards the friends when Alex had heard its noise. Maybe the animal did it to make itself look like a cave wall to them, owing to its size and skin texture. It might've been smart, camouflaging itself as a wall. The only thing that had given it away from its stealth activity was its noise. Now that the animal had seen them, the trio panicked and started running to get away from the beast. After running for a while, they spotted a tree and immediately climbed it. Even though it was hard to find a straight, upright tree on the island, they managed to find one in the middle of nowhere. Angelina had the most trouble climbing the tree, so Alex and Lester helped her climb.

'This awful girl always has problems, earlier with the luggage and now with the monkey skills. Really, monkey climbing isn't our type,' said Alex mockingly.

'Can't you just keep your mouth shut for a while, mister joker?' Angelina retorted.

'Okay, okay,' Alex replied, still retaining a hint of smile on his face. Turning towards Lester he continued, 'Um, are we so skilled and competent to leave a dangerous wild animal behind, destroying all its hope to feast upon us? I am quite certain that it'll come looking for us again. These are huge animals; our plan cannot succeed so easily unless...' said Alex.

'Unless?' asked Lester.

'See, that huge animal in the cave couldn't succeed in making any of us its prey, which is unbelievable. But, I guess it hasn't given up still. It might have told its family about us, and how the three of us were supposed to be their lunch. So, all in all, I think they would try to find us. I mean, I guess so,' Alex looked confused and uncertain about his thoughts.

'That would be our bad luck, I suppose,' said Lester.

The Weird Island

Suddenly, Alex noted that this experience could serve as a perfect storyline for a school play. It didn't seem real at all. 'Smart, sharp and peculiar animals... prey... family treat...' muttered Alex. A little later, he realized that in his nervous state, he had resorted to interpret the unusual incidents in a lighter vein in order to remain upbeat in the face of looming dangers.

'What I'm trying to believe is that the animal is huge but a doofus, lacking skills or intelligence,' he added.

'That would be our good luck, I suppose,' replied Lester with a broad smile, joking again.

'I think we're safe, unless the beast comes again...' said Angelina with a wry expression on her face.

Alex was hungry, and thirsty too. After the shock of the emergency landing, he wasn't feeling too good. At last, when he knew that they were safe, he became aware that he hadn't eaten for a long time. His friends too shared the same plight, and were desperate to eat something.

Luckily, the tree they had climbed had high branches and bore fruits, which resembled an apple.

'Another strange species, now of trees, huh. Apples don't grow on high trees. This is a new kind of fruit,' Alex said. 'First, lemme check, whether they are edible or not.'

He knew it was a risky task. Nevertheless, he bit a little part of the fruit. It tasted like cherry and litchi mixed together. When he didn't feel any kind of abnormality, he gave the green signal to Lester and Angelina.

All of them helped themselves to the fruits.

'*Dish ish reeeully tashty, bro*,' said Lester, still chewing.

'See what I got here,' added Lester, pulling out some small water bottles from Angelina's handbag. They gulped down the water quickly, relieving their parched mouths and quenching their thirst at last.

'These bottles are *too* less in number. What're we gonna do when these are finished? Obviously, we can't drink sea water,' Angelina expressed her thoughts.

'We'll think about that later, assuming we live long enough to finish these water bottles,' replied Alex.

The condition of the trio was not good. They had just finished their first meal. Tired of running and hiding, they desperately required some rest. But, the tree was not a comfortable place. They decided to climb down and move further.

The Weird Island

While they were climbing off the tree, they encountered a whole family of another species of wild animal. It was not from the honoereon family.

Alex was the first to point it to his friends, who were still not vigilant. The family appeared to be ferocious, but didn't attack any of them. It brought them unexpected joy to know that not all animals on the island were harmful. Its features were so peculiar. It was camouflage-coloured, and whenever the herd of animals stopped at a particular spot for more than five seconds, they disappeared into the surroundings. 'This strangeness... is there no end of it? This is just gonna get me to... but it's good that these don't seem harmful. Anyway, now what?' wondered Alex.

But, their joy was short-lived. Unaware of the next set of troubles waiting for them on this confusing, mysterious and peculiar island, they continued to move on. Suddenly, another weird and huge animal herd ran towards them. It was fierce and appeared desperate to attack. 'Yeah, now that's the honoereon family. Run!' said Alex.

As he glanced around his surroundings, Alex spotted a cave-like entity nearby, camouflaged by bushes.

'Quickly! In there!' he yelled, pointing towards the cave.

All three of them rushed in before the pack of strange animals could get to them. The cave was like a tunnel. Fortunately, it was not big enough to fit any of the animals who were chasing them. Not even the children of their species could fit in. Only the three of them were small enough to get inside it. They were now safe from the wild animals but their troubles weren't over yet.

'Another cavern? Well, how do we get out of this "Cavernal Mess" eh?' said Lester.

Alex had began to feel a little drowsy by that time. He was tensed, too.

But despite this, driven by his instincts he replied grumpily, 'Seems like a passageway to me... You know what Lester, just walk through the tunnel and you'll get out of your "Cavernal Mess"...'

They strode their way inside the cave. After about half an hour, they reached at the end of the tunnel. What they saw was an altogether different world—a peculiar, mysterious and interesting world, a world quite different from the human one, a world run by strange animals belonging to the two species they'd seen on the other part of the island.

There were multiple man-made ancient buildings on either side of the streets, which were partially broken down and ruined. The construction and architecture were similar to ancient Asian buildings. The damaged monuments appeared to have served in the past as residential houses and recreational centres, thus depicting that the place was equipped with the basic infrastructure that a well-developed city needs. Alex, who stood on a high cliff at a point where the cave ended, got a good view of the place. He was somewhat sad and shocked to find a magnificent historical city broken, ruined, rampaged. It appeared that the deadly creatures acted as if the city were theirs. They not only destroyed the city but were also living in the half-broken houses.

'Hey, look there. Those buildings are huge. They are partially broken. They might've been encroached and damaged by these creatures. They might even think of this place as "home", but they do not deserve to have a residence. It's hard to speculate what had happened here. And how did these beasts get to own this place? Our fate has already led us here. I wonder what *our* destiny will be...' Alex presumed and questioned at the same time in a shocked state, though knowing that there was no answer to his questions.

'This place is... gross,' said Angelina. 'Do we have to live at the mercy of these animals? Or... befriend them? Or... get killed?'

'Befriending them isn't possible. How can you even *think* of something as ridiculous as *that*?'

'Really?' Angelina raised an eyebrow.

'No offence, okay? Let's figure out someplace to stay. We can't possibly roam around the streets, waiting for these animals to kill us.'

'Nah, of course not. Anyway, wanna have an apple-litchi fruit?' Lester asked, still joking.

'Yup, let's move on,' replied Alex, accepting a fruit from Lester.

\..\... `'

Chapter 4

The Rough Rescue Plan and the First Day on the Island

Meanwhile, in Florida, the parents of the three friends were getting worried as they could not establish any contact with their children. The time to reach Japan had elapsed long back, and uncertainty led to unpleasant thoughts hovering around their minds.

'Lester would have kept his phone on flight mode and forgotten to switch it back to the normal mode,' his mother assumed. Parents of Alex and Angelina had no such assumptions, as both were not careless like Lester. Plus, they knew that if the children had landed, they would have been able to contact their parents, as there was no chance of NO SIGNAL in a developed country like Japan. They suspected some mishap.

As time passed by, they became more and more anxious. Frustrated and depressed, they called for a meeting at the Drakes residence.

Eric, Lester's father, suggested, 'I didn't receive any response from the airlines... I think we don't have any other choice but to call the cops and get information on what's really going on. If something happens to them... Then?'

'Don't worry. We'll see to it,' said Angelina's father, Clinton.

'But, how do we get to know the status of the plane and the people on board?' interrupted Clive, Alex's father.

Alex's mother Lucy called out for everyone's attention by announcing, 'I think Eric is right about calling the police. Maybe we could get some information from them. Let's try it, Clinton...'

'Um... okay, then.'

Everyone agreed.

The police reported within half an hour at Mr Drake's place. There were two cops. One of them was a big, muscular man, who seemed to be a senior officer of the Florida Police.

The Rough Rescue Plan and the First Day on the Island

The other cop, a bearded man with short, curly hair, stated nonchalantly, with a *none of our business* look on his face, 'The plane has disappeared at a spot near the Puerto Rico Trench and the Bermuda Triangle in North Atlantic Ocean... We have no clue yet'.

Suddenly, it seemed as if a strong current had passed through the two officers. They vibrated a bit while standing, as if they were possessed or hypnotized. Not knowing what and how this happened, the trio's parents looked at them awestruck.

A second later, the cops acted as if nothing had happened. 'Are you both okay?' Eric asked, but the policemen didn't reply. Both the officers stood still, like a statue. The bearded cop continued, 'And... if we're right... Precisely, we can say that the plane has disappeared near the most dangerous island of the world—Wasor Island, which is unknown to almost the whole world. Anyway, we have no more information yet.'

All six of them froze. They were too shocked to be able to utter anything.

At that very instant, the senior cop got a call on his walkie-talkie. He excused himself and took the call, moving a bit away from the lot. While conversing, his lips seemed to quiver.

'Sir, we have not received any information about the passengers and the crew till now; the search is going on,' the other cop said hesitatingly, looking towards the impatiently waiting parents. 'Earlier too, several aircrafts got lost in the vicinity of the Bermuda Triangle; the whereabouts of those aircrafts couldn't be traced. What I mean to say is... There's no clue... There is no news about the aircraft yet...'

The senior cop approached everyone as he ended his call. He reported, with a *I pity you people* look on his face, that the plane had actually made a water landing near Wasor Island. As per the information he had received, the aircraft encountered a technological glitch, which forced an emergency landing.

'Since then, there is no track of the people in the plane. Only the co-pilot has been rescued, who had reported witnessing a killer whale attacking some of the passengers and possibly those who were heading towards the island near the aircraft,' he ended.

The parents were shocked to hear this. Despite their nervousness, they thanked the cops and allowed them to leave.

'I can only pray that Alex, Lester and Angelina have been spared by the whale,' said Clive, who appeared to be uneasy and jittery.

The Rough Rescue Plan and the First Day on the Island

Eric added quickly, 'We must do something to rescue them.'

Hearing this, Susan, Angelina's mother, hesitatingly questioned, 'But how will we...? We aren't even sure of their presence on that very island.'

Finally, Lester's mother Isabella took the lead and announced, 'We can do it and we have to do it. By planning meticulously and executing courageously, we should be able to rescue our children. Let's keep our hopes alive.'

Everyone appreciated Eric and Isabella's courage and mental strength, and started thinking of the ways to overcome the family crisis.

| Wasor |

At the island, the three friends were trying to find a safe place to stay. After walking for hours, they were extremely hungry.

'Thanks to the dangerous animal, we discovered the fruit-laden tree. We have quite in store at present,' said Lester.

Soon, another trouble was staring them right in the face. A little one of those peculiar animals came running towards the trio and started staring at them, its face revealing that it found the humans to be strange. This was not surprising given that on the island it was the animals who reigned supreme.

Before they knew it, there was not only one animal staring at them, but tens of them. They couldn't anticipate whether those animals were harmful or not, but could only hope that they did not attack them. They had to make a tough decision.

'Either we should give up hope and surrender as prey to these animals, or... we should start accepting our days of struggle and forced adventure in this peculiar and mysterious world.' Alex mused in his *brainy* but sometimes crazy mind.

Lester said, 'Um, what do you seriously think we must do now? Get killed by these CC?'

'Carbon copy? What're you talking about?' said Alex.

'Get killed by these creepy creatures, or CC for short,' replied Lester, apparently amused by Alex's funny suggestions.

'Quickly, run! These animals aren't gonna leave us alive,' commanded Alex.

'This man keeps ordering,' said Angelina sarcastically, subsequently following her running friends.

The Rough Rescue Plan and the First Day on the Island

After running for a while, Alex was forced to stop. His legs were itching as they came in contact with the piercing acidic and pungent-smelling grass. Alex then found a place to hide behind a rock in a grassland. Staying there for about 2 minutes, he realized that the rock wasn't really a rock. It was moving slowly. Blackish brown in colour, its outer surface was as hard as a rock. But when it suddenly moved, they knew that it was another one of those strange creatures.

'Another beast belonging to an alien species... Let's move on before it slays us,' Angelina exclaimed, alarmed. All three of them quickly took off from that spot.

Their search for a safe place to hide continued. The time spent in these new surroundings was quite uncomfortable for Alex. 'It might not be so *disastrous* for Lester, cause he might still be tickling his funny bone all the time,' Alex thought looking at Lester, who was still in a funny mood, cracking jokes to Angelina.

After wandering for hours, they found an abandoned palace.

'I wonder who built this mansion at this island,' Angelina was curious.

'Incredible,' Alex thought as he got a new idea to add to his storyline school play. 'Let's stay in this mansion. Though the building has been abandoned, at least it will give us a refuge to hide.'

'How safe is it? What if it's haunted?' asked Angelina.

'Come on Angelina. Don't get all of your "imaginations" bundled up together again. Be realistic, there are no signs of creepiness in this manor house. Just get it off your mind that this place is haunted. We have just seen that your... um...perceptions are not always correct. That animal didn't stand a chance against us.'

'Look who is talking. Did you forget that we didn't *fight* it? We just escaped like cowards,' replied an insulted Angelina. Alex remained silent, knowing that he was beaten in his own game.

'It's such an old architecture. It withstood time and didn't get destroyed, even by these animals. There might be something special about it. Let's go inside and see how it looks...' said Lester.

Angelina raised an eyebrow.

'This mansion appears to be built by humans to remain safe from the creatures of this place. That's why I think that this is the safest place on this island for us. Plus, none of the strange animals could get inside, as the doors are constructed in such a way that only humans can enter through it. The animals here are too big to enter into any such buildings, even the smallest ones. No one appears to be living here. Anyway, let's head in,' Alex spoke, ending his friend's debate.

Lester and Angelina discussed Alex's idea and agreed to follow his advice. Without further delay, they entered the mansion and noticed that it was completely ruined. Window panes were broken; the front gate, which might've been a huge magnificent metal door once, now lay in scraps.

Once inside, Alex didn't seem to be satisfied by his interpretation about the existence of the mansion. Multiple questions buzzed through his mind.

The three friends strode their way forward into the monument, walking silently through the mysterious and magnanimous building.

The huge front yard of the mansion contained dried patches of grass here and there. There was a dry water fountain in front of the steps that led to the main entrance (Alex didn't even try to think how the people managed a water fountain *that* long back. Of course everything was too *weird*). But it was clear that this place had been abandoned long back.

As Alex entered the building, he realized that making a magnificent mansion like this wasn't a child's play. It must've been magnificent and grand when it was inhabited and in use.

Alex walked towards the dilapidated rectangular metal door, pushing it with all his might, his friends helping him in his effort. Once the door was open, he saw a large front lobby, dusty and ruined. Moving a little further, they reached a T-point.

As Alex was about to turn left, Lester took him by the hand and said, 'Right is always right.'

Alex then gestured Angelina to follow them to the right. Compared to the wide muddy path road outside the monument, the path inside was relatively narrow. Soon, he came across a large room in front of him, filled with multiple chairs and tables, all broken, torn and destroyed. The whole room appeared to have been rampaged by rats and insects, with cushions of the chairs chewed on and stale food strewn on the floor. There were several other rooms on the side, perhaps used as meeting rooms for different purposes.

After exploring for a while, they entered another huge room—the biggest they had seen so far. It looked grand and imposing. There was a high platform on which the king's large throne was placed. Around it were more seats, arranged in a semicircle.

'For the courtiers, I think. These surrounding chairs might've been for them. I see scraps of metal on the ground. This might've been the boundaries; the boundaries for the people to signify the king's supremacy and the grace of his throne in the courtroom,' thought Alex.

'Look, there is a garden there,' said Angelina excitedly.

The big hall was adjacent to a garden, which was still green. Alex was surprised to find an artificial canal, which still carried water for the plants.

'Perhaps this canal receives water diverted from a natural stream. The internal gravity-based automated irrigation system of the canal has kept the garden green even now,' he said, mesmerized by the amazing planning.

'What I say is, I wanna be the king of this place... *if* it's maintained properly. Then, I gotta be frolicking all day in this garden. Some servants to keep up to my demands... And it's done,' exclaimed Lester.

'Not so quick, my dear king. Wait. We haven't even explored half of the mansion until now,' said Alex.

Alex looked all around the garden. He noticed a two-storeyed, ruined building. It was completely destroyed, with stones crumbling down now and then.

'No need to head there. We cannot risk getting buried under stones. Let's follow the canal. Maybe that'll lead us to another part of the mansion. But first let's find a place to rest. I'm really tired,' said Alex, deciding on the next plan of action.

As they followed the little canal, it led them to a large rectangular dried-up depression on the ground.

'A pool, huh. This is just *sooo*... relaxing, isn't it? Poor we, everything's just *ruined* here,' said Angelina.

The canal continued further to faraway lands, but they didn't wish to follow it anymore. There was another passageway to the left. They went through it and found a few two-storeyed buildings on both its sides. Inside were residential rooms, but there was no proper place to rest. The rooms were ruined, too, with scraps of objects lying on the floor, including fluffs of cushion feathers.

The Rough Rescue Plan and the First Day on the Island

There was also a rough, spiral stone staircase in the corner, which led upstairs.

Angelina shuddered and thanked Alex, 'This place looks creepy. I bet it'll seem worse in the night. But... gee, thanks, Alex, for spotting a place for shelter.'

Alex replied, 'Never mind. My wristwatch indicates 7 p.m. right now. I think we should hurry and find a better place to rest.' They climbed up the stairs and found three rooms on the floor. In the first room was a shabby king-size bed, while a rickety queen size one was kept in the other room. There were ruins of beds, cushions, and wood and ripped leather from a couch in the third one, spread all around like garbage.

'This place is too bad for stay,' Lester complained.

'The mansion is not as magnificent as it appears to be from the outside, Lester. You can see that it is covered in cobwebs and surrounded by creepy crawlies. Rats have eaten the soft, cushiony seats, while the rest of the monument has been destroyed by the animals,' Alex reasoned.

'We can move somewhere else if you guarantee to find a place that is safer than this,' Alex added at last, after reading Lester's *Kill me now* expression. Maybe he really didn't like reasoning or sound arguments.

'Umm... nah,' Lester and Angelina replied in unison.

Without wasting time (as he always tended to do), Alex opted for the king-size bed, and Angelina for the queen-size one. But poor Lester had no choice but to sleep in the third room.

'No way! I don't like a mess where I sleep. I'm gonna spend the night with you in *your* room. If you aren't happy with this solution, then at least try to do something about it,' Lester told Alex in one go, as they did their best to clean up the rooms for the night.

'You're on.'

'Thanks, man,' said Lester, giving him a thumbs up.

After settling down, they ate the packets of junk food which Angelina carried in her purse. They drank water from the packaged water bottles they had brought as their hand baggage. Since their cell phones were wet due to swimming in the sea, Lester tried to repair it by drying them up, but they didn't work. Alex was scared suspecting the impossibility of their parents to contact them.

'But... but... wait a minute. D'ya wholly guarantee that this place is safe? I know none of the animals can get in. But what if there's something else...?' Angelina asked Alex.

The Rough Rescue Plan and the First Day on the Island

'I guess we'll have to be on our toes to detect any signs of danger. Let's explore the place, and if anyone of us finds or suspects something, we could whistle loudly to draw attention. Okay?'

'Okay,' Angelina and Lester agreed.

As Alex moved up through the spiral staircase, he saw a symbol, etched in the wall so perfectly as if by a machine.

'There appears to be some inscriptions on it, but they're kind of awkward... A symbol, so deeply carved... and they're fine curves... What's all this?' Alex thought doubtfully.

The search continued, but nothing dangerous could be found. But at the end of the search, Lester and Angelina claimed to have seen the same symbol at two different spots in the mansion.

After Alex's first day on the island, he needed a good night's sleep to recover from the disastrous and heartbreaking day. So he slept early at 8 p.m. by his watch, without bothering to find out whether his comrades had slept or were finding it difficult to fall asleep.

\..\... `'

Chapter 5

The Traces of the Mystery

The sun was up when Alex woke. He saw Lester, who was sleeping beside him. He went out of his room to check whether Angelina was awake. He knocked on Angelina's door, but got no answer. Then he thought of waking Lester up to plan the day, but then something stopped him. He remembered the question that arose in his mind regarding the man-made mansion on this Penimal-inhabited island, as named by Alex in reference to the peculiar animals.

He started exploring the mansion to find clues to his questions.

He went downstairs, where he observed carefully the throne of the king and the rat-eaten cushioned chairs. He remembered his archaeologist friend who had taught him a few archaeology skills. Minutely, he observed each corner. He saw some text, which appeared to be embossed on a stone surface, embedded on a three-feet tall square-shaped pillar, beside the throne on the right. The script inscribed on it appeared similar to the Vedic language, which he had seen on another thick, grime-covered stone plate, inscribed on an isolated three-feet tall stone pillar at the entrance. A similar script was seen embedded at another place on the floor, which was strewn with rubbles. He unsoiled it and started reading. Despite all his efforts, he couldn't understand it. He tried hard to remember all that his friend from India had explained to him. But he had only learnt the basics years ago. In the end, he could understand only one word in the heading—*Sabhamandapaha*, which means assembly hall. This was enough for him to figure out that the throne and the chairs formed the seating arrangement of the king and his courtiers in the judicial court, a place where official meetings were conducted.

Now Alex understood that a human populace existed on the island long ago.

The Traces of the Mystery

But there were more questions in his mind. 'How come these unheard and weird animals are here? What happened to the humans? How did it happen? Really, I'm starting to transform my brain into a ball of slush with all these puzzles in my mind.'

Before he knew it, he was called by Lester. He was upstairs looking for Alex in the room but was shocked on not finding him there.

'Hey, Alex, just needed to ask y–Alex... Alex? Alex! Buddy! WHERE IS HE? HAVE THE MONSTERS EATEN 'IM UP–,' he was yelling before Alex showed up upstairs with a grin on his face.

Lester was relieved to find his friend. Alex told him the facts he unearthed from the script.

Lester listened carefully, and soon questions started popping up like popcorn in his mind, too. He panted as he expressed his views, just like Alex did before he had figured out about the assembly hall.

Then, they decided to plan the day with Angelina and subsequently knocked on her door. No answer.

Lester and Alex joked, 'Maybe she is out cold,' and laughed out loudly, which eventually woke Angelina.

She walked out of her room and screamed angrily at both of them, 'Are you both trying to blow off my eardrums?' Though they apologized, they quietly exchanged mocking gestures between them.

Lester told Angelina about Alex's discovery. She had always aspired to become an archaeologist, and was thrilled to hear the news. Now, she was even more eager to gather further knowledge about the mysterious island.

'Remember how she discussed ancient stuff all the time?' Alex asked Lester while Angelina was away, checking out the stone plate.

'Yup. Those were hard days, listening to her nonsense all the time. I mean, there's *other* stuff to do in life, too. All the time she said the same things, huh. *Archaeologist*, she wanted to be? Really, she's kinda...'

'We really don't need another adjective for her qualities right now. You must not consider her as dull and boring, who only talks about things off the topic *nowadays*. She is grown up, you know. She is not that childish, at least not as earlier times. But you know, if she's angry she'll still throw tantrums around.'

'You seem right. So, as for now, I'm gonna *shut up.*'

Alex approached Angelina and asked her to join him and Lester, and start planning the day in order to survive. They had no food except for a few fruits and edibles in their bags. He reiterated her words that only one of the three water bottles was left and obviously they couldn't drink sea water. So, they now had to fetch water from the natural stream.

But Angelina wanted to investigate the mansion right away and didn't care about the planning.

'Once we leave this mansion, I don't think it would be easy to come back,' she said. 'None of us know our way around this island. So, let's not leave this opportunity to explore the old mansion.'

'Who knows what clues we will get from here,' she added quickly, demolishing some of Alex's hope about stalling her investigation. But not all.

Alex knew that this was not more important than keeping them alive and tried to get her out of the mansion. But, it did no good. She wouldn't budge no matter how hard he tried, even though he was supported by Lester. At last, Alex and Lester found themselves investigating the mansion for more clues. As they were looking it up, brushing off the dust from the objects, Alex heard strange noises coming from outside.

| Florida |

'I suggest few of us should go to the island to find and rescue them. We must hire an aeroplane for the same and bring them back,' Clinton was the first to speak up.

Clive suggested that he has his own chartered plane, which could be used rather than hiring one. Everybody agreed to his proposal.

Now, the question arose regarding who would go on this rescue operation.

'Don't we need to take help of the police?' Isabella doubted.

Clive said, 'That place is a no man's land and outside the territory of our nation. I guess the cops will not like to get involved in it. Some of us, I presume, Clinton, Eric and me, would be heading there. But we'll need some support...'

Eric opined that the Army shall certainly help them. Clive reacted positively and took out his mobile phone. He made a call, then excused himself and conversed with the person for a while.

As he hung up the call, he told everyone, 'I have just spoken to the Secretary of the Defence Minister, who is my close friend. He has assured that we may get Army support. Clive, you need not take any pain regarding the mode of transport. We're all set. Let's prepare the rescue plan, and get ready accordingly.'

\..\... `'

Chapter 6

The Terrific Mystery

| Wasor |

The strange noises emanating from outside the mansion seemed dangerous. Alex went to shut the door so that he could block the disturbing sounds.

After closing the door, as he looked back towards the wall facing the door, he found a ghastly creature standing in front of him. It was a vague, dark green jelly-like humanoid. Alex was startled and horrified by this paranormal creature. Alarmed, he took a step back, careful of his every move, while keeping a vigil on the astonishing creature, which appeared to have jumped out from the *Conjuring* movies. It wore a black hoodie jacket with tattered jet-black pants. Deadly metal spikes covered the surface of his cloth, preventing one from getting too close and cause him any harm. It bore ancient inscriptions on the head, which, if, translated into English, may read, 'Hey, your death here! Wanna have some fun?' guessed Alex. Its eyes were multi-coloured like a kaleidoscope, comprising dark green, black, *really* dark blue and dark red colours, which seemed to hypnotize Alex. It was as if the creature wanted Alex to keep staring at him. The ghoul growled at Alex like... um... your most horrific and frightening dream growls at you.

Alex didn't believe in ghosts, but after seeing such a creature, anyone could become a scaredy cat. Though he was frightened and his senses were at fever pitch, he didn't lose his calm. Patiently, he started moving towards his friends, whom he had left in their respective rooms, not breaking the insecure eye contact with that creature. But, soon Alex felt something extraordinary about that ghoul. It seemed to be sapping away his energy from him. He started to feel exhausted. And just as he blinked after maintaining eye contact all this while, the creature vanished.

That very moment, he rushed towards his friends, who were out of their rooms by then and told them about his escapade. He was still terrified, and tried his best to explain the incident. He also warned them that this place was quite dangerous, and they should move away as soon as possible. Of course, they didn't believe him. But being good friends, they pretended to trust him.

'But in their furtive minds, I just *know*, they are still doubtful about my narration. They're surely thinking that I'm mad,' thought Alex as he observed their traits, trying to judge their thoughts.

Lester expressed his views on the matter when Angelina was out of earshot, 'It was probably your imagination. The tiredness due to the unexpected and exhaustive experiences on this island might have caused it. You must chill, bro. Let's assume nothing like that ever took place.'

Angelina, on the other hand, pitied the poor boy who was daydreaming. She attempted to mock him, but seeing the sensitivity of the situation, retracted her action. However, noticing her unusual behaviour, Alex got a hint of her attempted mockery.

'Hmph! That's what *they* think', he muttered to himself.

'His friends waited to let this blow over in his mind and get him back from "daydreamomania",' Alex continued to draft his screenplay in his mind. From then on, he had decided to make it a screenplay rather than a school drama play. 'Drama is kinda old-fashioned and boring. Screenplay is like... involving a movie theatre? Yeah, it's much better,' he thought as he tried to distract himself from the memory of the ghost.

Alex was fed up of being humiliated by his friends, and decided to utilize his time better. So, he told them to cut off the ongoing nonsense and plan the day, as they had no food and very less water left for the day. He instructed them to join him in search of food. Since he was older than them and had saved their lives—not once, but twice—they had to respect his decision. After all, he was the one who made them get out of the "Cavernal Mess" and also made the tough decision of fighting the trouble in this peculiar world.

The trio headed out of the mansion, with Alex succeeding in making them completely forget about the useless investigation of the mansion. As they moved on, they came to know about the source of those dangerous noises. They witnessed a fight between two animals of the island, which reminded Alex of a wrestling match on WWF. It was as if two dinosaurs had escaped from Jurassic Park and were fighting out in the open. Alex noticed the presence of an *animal audience* too. He signalled his friends to crouch as low as possible, and escape whenever they found a chance. They then hid behind the penimals' stinking rough brown backs, not forgetting to block their noses with their hands, and slowly moved away from the spot.

Having walked a long distance, approximately two to three kilometres from the 'audience', they were still not completely devoid of danger. Their bad luck had bound them to the animals' world, just like flesh is bound to bones, which *could* be torn apart, but with great pain and difficulty.

At that moment, there were very few animals on that part of the island. Alex could observe this world minutely, unhindered by those tall and humongous creatures who obstructed the view. The place looked different from the rest of the island. Though he was no archaeologist, he could sense traces of human civilization here, as if humans once lived on this island. 'Or, probably, still do...' Alex's eyes sparkled but grew dim immediately. The very thought of human life

The Terrific Mystery

gave him hope, yet he was also apprehensive. 'What if those humans were not friendly? What if they were barbarous?' he wondered.

At some distance, in between the large trees, whose bases were covered by bushes, they saw remains of an altogether different kind of architecture. It was difficult to guess who built it and for what purpose. It seemed as if it were another building made by humans, and was destroyed by the penimals later. Suddenly, Angelina seemed to remember something. '*Now* I do recall that I had forced you two to investigate the mansion... and after the *Alex Madman* incident I had forgotten everything. Ugh! I've been forced into this thing, but... never mind. Now I can investigate not only the mansion but also this whole peculiar world. And *sorry* Alex, for calling you a madman,' she told the boys, though her tone wasn't really apologetic, and was rather sarcastic.

'A long speech as per your standard, girl,' Alex replied, making fun of her.

Annoyed by such a response, she bumped him on the back with her fist in a friendly way.

'Oww... that hurt. Easy, okay? Otherwise...' he teased her.

Just as he thought that Angelina would have a clever comeback, her expression changed from cunning to shocked, as she gazed at a particular direction. She was pointing towards something. 'There,' she said.

When the other two looked towards it, they saw an adult human hand behind a ruined building, which was plopped down on the ground. A person was supposedly sitting at a corner of the building. However, he was on the other side and hence not visible.

The hand was like a treasure for the trio on this island. But they didn't know whether the hand was for real. What was significant to them wasn't the fleshy and dirt-coated hand, but the person *whose* hand it was. He could provide them with a lot of information. Alex started doubting this because humans could hardly survive on the island for more than, say, a week? Two days? A day?

Alex and his friends ran towards the hand. They saw a man, plopped down on the ground near the building. He was unconscious. He looked like an Indian, and wore an ancient society's clothes, as described by Domingo Paes who visited the Vijayanagara Empire. The outfit was dirty and appeared as if it had been pooped on.

He was covered in layers and layers of grime, much like the mansion on the island. He smelled awful. His eyelids appeared bruised and blue, and his face was quite attractive, even though he was quite old and his skin had wrinkled.

'Is he alive?' asked Lester.

'Another passenger from our flight, I think,' Angelina presented her thoughts.

'He's alive, I think. Let's search him, what if he's a threat to us...?' said Alex.

Alex couldn't believe it. At first he thought the man could be one of the passengers from the flight. But, by the looks of his clothes, he appeared unusual and different. Moreover, if such an old man were travelling with them, there was a high possibility of being noticed by at least one of them.

'Dunno whether he is a fellow passenger. Doesn't appear to be anyone from our flight,' said Lester while searching the man.

'Wonder who is he,' exclaimed Angelina.

'If he is someone else, then how long has he been on this island? Being so old and weak, how is he surviving and for how long has he been surviving...' questions like these were taking space in Alex's mind.

This person was their only hope. Alex expected some help from this man. But in his present condition, he didn't seem to be in a state to help anyone. Instead, he himself needed medical aid. Slowly, he gained consciousness, but was extremely weak. He lay on the ground and just managed to croak a word out of his mouth, which none of them could understand.

Slightly reluctant, yet out of excitement and hope, Alex started by asking him, 'Who're you, what's your–,' but stopped looking at the man's state of helplessness. He then asked his friends to help him take the man to the mansion. He also told them that they might be able to find answers to their queries from this stranger.

They soon reached the mansion, as the *animal audience* had cleared out. Alex led them to his king-size bed and said, 'Put him here. Yeah, that's it. Now bring me a water bottle.'

They plopped him on the ancient bed as fast as possible, as they didn't want to touch the filthy robe for long. Alex hadn't paid much attention to his clothes earlier, but Angelina observed his dress minutely. He was wearing a dusty, ragged and almost half-stripped crimson robe.

Lester brought him a water bottle from the remaining three.

Alex splashed some water on the man's face, not caring about the shortage of water they faced. Plus, he thought that once they get help from this man, he could lead them to the source of essentials on this island. He intuitively suspected that this stranger knew all about the place. He could also help them in their hunt, as they weren't in a position to kill those huge animals for food. But, Alex figured out that if the man had been surviving for a long time, he must know where to find edibles.

After Alex sprinkled water on his face, the man became more aware of his surroundings. He was still not fully conscious, and muttered under his breath, 'Animals…killing…destruction…Khagaha…' he paused, gasping for breath. '…Vadhaha…Dashaha…Dandaha,' he went on murmuring, before falling unconsciousness again.

Alex realized that this man needed nutrition and energy before he could be of any assistance to them. In a subconscious state, he was speaking in some other language, but it appeared that he knew English well. Maybe he wasn't able to process the scene or his words. They had to find food for this poor man. Alex asked, 'Get me *human* edible food from somewhere. Whether from your bag, Angelina, or... from anywhere else. I just need something for this poor fellow.'

As he noticed his friends' subdued *Oh, really? Can't you be polite and a bit less bossy?* facial expressions, he lowered his tone. 'I mean... this man could prove helpful to us. Please go and find something to eat, no matter how hard you have to work for it, and be *quick* please.'

Lester and Angelina then went off in search of a nutritional source.

Alex sat waiting, beside the unidentified person, on an old, dusty rocking chair. A moment later, he gazed up in shock, as he saw the ghost again; this time it was floating around the ceiling.

He sat there, watching cautiously. He was terrified. A moment before he was sitting comfortably and resting, and a second later he felt he was not just there, but was rather *petrified* by the ghost. Suddenly, he turned into a miniature-size statue made up of jet-black marble.

His arms and legs froze, his consciousness froze, and soon, his eyes froze too. Everything was dark

The Terrific Mystery

around him, until he heard a scream, which sounded like Angelina's. His little marble statue hardened, thus compressing his mind and his hope.

Later, Alex woke up and found himself in the middle of a forest. Bent over him were Angelina and Lester, observing him carefully, with eyes full of hope. He stood up, looked around and saw the old man, who now looked better and healthy, slurping juice from a fruit resembling a mango.

Alex asked, 'Wha–what happened...? I only recall myself sitting on a chair and...uh! From then on I don't seem to remember! Some dream... was it? The cracking sound of a hardening stone, a scream...'

Lester put his hand on Alex's shoulder and said patiently, 'Sit, we'll tell you the whole story,' Alex sat up straight and listened attentively.

Lester explained, 'Listen, we were wrong about the existence of that mysterious ghost. We're really sorry for making fun of you; it *does* exist. When we returned to the mansion with fruits, we saw that you were turning into a solid black marble. We also spotted that ghost. Angelina screamed in horror, but we didn't waste time like you did while trying to keep a tab on the ghost.'

Alex hated being called a time-waster since he was punctual enough compared to them. He scowled at Lester. 'Go on.'

Lester continued, 'We rushed out of the haunted place with your small statue, successively halting here in the forest. We've got the answers...they are really disturbing...' Alex cut him off and said, 'But how did I come back to my normal state?'

Lester replied, 'You became you because we helped you.'

Alex's expression changed to like *What? Have you gone mad? Speak in detail, fella.* He was getting impatient and wanted to know the details.

Angelina said, interrupting, 'When we touched you, the marble started to melt off, and slowly and gradually left your body. Apparently... one can get cured *only* by human touch. Thank goodness we're a group, not a solo traveller. Anyway, that's what Mr V told us.'

Alex understood that only human body warmth could heal another person from the wrath of that ghoul. He doubtfully, but eagerly, asked, 'What are the answers... Disturbing... Lester said...? Who's Mr V?'

The Terrific Mystery

'Mr V. Short for V-I-S-H-W-A-R-O-O-P-A-H-A. We spent 10 minutes trying to learn how to pronounce his name. Anyway, Mr V will tell you all we discussed. It's... unbelievable.'

That man started to speak, turning towards Alex, his brown eyes glowing. Alex saw his gleaming eyes, too, and he knew this wasn't his imagination. There seemed to be something unusual about that man. He said, 'Hi, my name is Vishwaroopaha Kanhesama. I will tell you all you need to know about this so-called paradise. I am an ancient Brahman, and was born in 473 BC. I mistakenly drank an unknown potion kept in a cave on the island, which was off-limits, not only for children, but also for adults. That liquid, when drunk by a person, could make him immortal—'

Alex was thrilled to hear about another form of chemistry other than alchemy that ancient people practised. He made a mental note to get it printed in the local newspaper when he got back home.

'Hey, he is about 2500 years older than all of us. At this island everything is so mysterious and unbelievable. It's even more incredible to find this particular oldie at such a weird island...heh!' thought Alex.

He looked at the old man again, observing him diligently this time.

'As he says, he is very old and by the looks of it, it really seems like he had been living for 2500 years or more. But on this island...? Is this possible?' he again remembered the ravaged human buildings at the island.

Putting aside all his thoughts, he started listening carefully to Mr Vishwaroopaha; Alex had found nothing difficult in his name.

He still felt there was something unusual about that man. Sometimes, Vishwaroopaha stopped while narrating his story. The pause almost always occurred whenever some thoughts crossed Alex's mind. Alex couldn't make out whether it was his facial expression while he was thinking something that made Vishwaroopaha stop his narration, or... could that man read Alex's mind?

He then looked approvingly towards his friends and continued listening, putting aside other thoughts. Vishwaroopaha continued, 'I'm not joking; one could really be immortal. I was just... unlucky. Death is essential, just as life. I have got this eternal grief of being immortal. I can't be put to death, and that's the problem. But... another benefit of that potion is that it prevented anyone to overpower me. Over the years, I have found out that I am invulnerable. No animal or human being can harm me; only the Divine has some effect on me. I don't usually brag about it since I *don't have* anyone to talk about my superior qualities... I'm just... broken... broken from within... No matter how many times these animals rip me apart, I heal fully. I am depressed... by all the bad fate this island has suffered. These animals are *really* cruel. I think you might've figured out that much by now. You can find human skeletons in each cave on this island, because of these murderous creatures... Why are they here, you might be wondering, aren't you? Alright... I'll be explaining shortly...'

Alex was amazed at this man's hope. He'd suffered a lot, but still he was sane. Most people in his situation would have become flesh-eaters or blood-thirsty cavemen, whereas this man seemed generous, and not merciless or savage. He didn't boast about his immortality. Instead he wanted death. 'Poor man,' thought Alex.

Vishwaroopaha stopped again, while Alex was lost in his thoughts. The man merely smiled. Alex didn't know why, but he still felt something was wrong about Vishwaroopaha. It seemed as if he weren't speaking the truth. 'But, yeah, he might be telling the truth. Lester had also found his story "unbelievable" at first. Let's listen further...' he thought.

Vishwaroopaha continued, 'The animals are here because of a strange curse inflicted on the residents of this island. Not many people know about this place, but it's been named Wasor Island. There used to be a Vedic kingdom here, but that powerful curse changed all the humans living here to these humongous, disgusting, destructive animals. I just find it hard to believe that the humans have been turned into these animals. You all might've thought of these animals as invaders and killers, but they're actually just those humans—*we* humans. That cave you all came through was once a passageway for humans only, but a day came when some of the humans were secretly turned into these peculiar animals. They destroyed the remaining human kingdom, took over and made a world of their own in 430 BC...'

He continued, 'Many of the ancient people's souls have become ghosts and haunt the old places here. The spirit who troubled you was my old friend, Vijaykarma.

The Terrific Mystery

And, then I was the one who told your friends the method to cure you.'

Lester and Angelina fidgeted, but Vishwaroopaha didn't seem to notice and continued carelessly, 'I know everything about this island. Ask me *anything* you want to know.'

Stunned, Alex stood there. There were about a thousand questions in his mind, but he realized that he wanted to become kind and generous like Vishwaroopaha, rather even better than him. He gathered himself, and of all the queries in his mind, he settled on asking only one, 'What can we do to cure these animals...umm...the ancient people?'

'It's a tough task, but I reckon that you can accomplish it. These animals were humans themselves, but the indigenous animals' king of that era inflicted a curse upon the humans and transformed them into animals. The curse extends to any person who tries but fails to return those animals back to their human form. What was the purpose of all this, I don't know. Maybe they just wanted to expand the population of their kind...'

He continued, his eyes having a persuasive effect on Alex, 'One who wishes to be the saviour of the people of this island has to get through a series of ten deadly challenges. You three must get through the challenges as if your life depends on it. There would be a lever at the end of the tenth challenge. Pull it down and see what happens. The first challenge is that mansion and its ghost Vijaykarma himself. And about that ruined mansion... I didn't enter that mansion because I didn't want to be turned into a marble statue, waiting for another human to help me. Sometimes friends can betray too, you know. So, I decided to wander around rather than... I think you should try to get through those challenges. By the way, I wish you good luck for the tasks. If you are in for the challenges, try not to get killed. They get harder and harder as you proceed further... I don't want to scare you, but... once you've taken them up, there's no turning back. You *have* to get through all ten of them or... die. Take enough food and water with you, because the task is going to last for *days*, not just hours. Anyway, bye for now!' Vishwaroopaha ended, and magically faded into the darkness before Alex had a chance to stop him and ask more questions.

Taken aback, Angelina asked doubtfully, in a trembling voice, 'Well, now what should we do? Do you really want to try it? The consequences may be harsh. Reconsider your choice. Whatever it is, we'll go with what you choose, because we know that you're the top-class survivor around here. The one who got himself turned into a figurine...' she ended mockingly.

Alex replied, 'Oh, shut up. I don't want to look back. I have decided to go for the challenge. Follow my lead. By the way, that man, Vishwaroopaha, is quite... suspicious. I think he can't be trusted. How did he even *know* English? He's an Indian—an ancient Indian. Let's see how genuine he is and how real his story of animals and curse is...'

'The only way to figure that out is to check whether the tasks he mentioned are for real...' Lester said.

'You're right. But that language thing... maybe it's due to the potion...' said Angelina.

'You seem right, too. But... he didn't mention anything about such... Anyway, for now, let's check out the challenges... I have a gut feeling that in case they truly exist... then... they aren't gonna be easy...' replied Lester.

They gathered some fruits for later, as it was the only food available. Soon, they found themselves facing the first challenge—the mansion and its ghost.

Chapter 7

The First Two Tasks

Alex stood in front of the mansion, amazed, aware of what fate had in store for them. Ten challenges. That's it. 'How hard could it be?' he thought. On one side of his mind courage reigned supreme, and on the other side there was nervousness and terror. Which one would he choose?

He didn't know how, but this time too, he chose the path of hope and courage, like he always did. And, off he went into the mansion, thinking *and* knowing that the first task would be to get past the ghost and then into a secret passage or trapdoor, which would lead them to the second task. He set off for the site where he had had read the word *Sabhamandapaha*,

The First Two Tasks

and was quietly followed by Lester and Angelina. He went to that spot because he figured that the inscriptions would give him some clue to the door, passageway or trapdoor, which would lead them to the next challenge, after they escape from the clutches of Vijaykarma. He was right. When he hovered his fingers over the inscription, the stone plate moved and crumbled into dust, leaving behind a door about ten times the size of the stone plate. 'Oh boy. This is interesting,' Lester said as he observed the process.

Alex scanned the solid golden door. This was the door to the secret passageway leading to the second task. He pushed the door open to reveal a soot-coated creaky staircase. He turned around to call his friends.

And then shockingly, he found out that right then both his friends had transformed into black marble statues. 'What the...' he realized it was the ghost again.

Just then, he saw that figure of Vijaykarma, floating right behind him. Quickly, he picked both the statues and climbed up the creaky stairs inside the golden gate.

After he woke them up in the manner he had learned from Lester, they found themselves in another extremely odd room. There was a shutter door at the other side of the room, just opposite the door through which he had entered. The place was quite dark. Nothing was visible except the shutter door, because of translucent glowing red light emanating from the bottom left corner. The room's walls were covered by a thick and strong metal mesh. It seemed like a garage, except that there were no cars or tools inside.

Suddenly, without giving him enough time to adjust to the surroundings, the shutter opened and out came around fifteen visible pairs of dark red glowing eyes, which were gleaming amidst the darkness. Alex suspected that these were the ghosts haunting *this* room. 'I don't believe Vishwaroopaha. That ghost couldn't possibly be his friend. He might've been one from this group... But... these *challenges* are turning out to be real...' Alex thought as he saw those eyes. Using flint rocks, he started a fire and lit the wood he'd brought from the forest. That's when he found out that those weren't ghosts, but... wolves. Precisely—joined wolves. They were all joined by the tail and the ear, with one wolf's tail joined to the ear of the next one. It was a pack of wolves, joined together to form one beast—a Multiwolf.

The First Two Tasks

As Alex saw them, they howled loudly, so loud that he started doubting that *his* eardrums would blow off.

But, unfortunately, the howling made the fire go out. The gust of air heading out from those creature's mouths extinguished the fire. The friends were surrounded by darkness again, save for the light emanating from the creature's eyes.

Right then, Lester reached over to his backpack and pulled out a mid-sized halogen searchlight. Once he lit it up, he positioned it at a certain angle, ensuring that the whole scene was clearly visible. He smiled and shouted over to Alex, showing him the light, 'Yo bro, I thought that you outta get some light to defeat that thing. So you have now. Go on.'

Alex managed to pass a faint smile. He knew that Lester was a jolly man; he would be smiling under any circumstances. As for himself, he felt proud to have managed a smile in that situation.

He faced the wolves again. 'This is the second challenge—The Multiwolf and its howls,' Alex named the challenge.

Alex suspected that the third challenge was at the back of the room, which was guarded by the shutter and the Multiwolf. He had to get past this creature somehow and cross the shutter to move to the next challenge. Besides, it now seemed that the Multiwolf was forming a tree-like structure, as the wolves started to join together in the form of a...tree—a coconut tree. 'A coconut...tree. What is it with coconuts and wolves? These wolves are up to something,' he thought after seeing the creature in the shape of a tree.

'Is this a funny joke or something to...trap us...? If not, then... what's it?' he thought, this time gathering himself.

Suddenly, the tree squeezed and bent to form a Beyblade. The wolves' faces jutted out of the spherical shape like spikes. 'Beyblade? Is this gonna spin me out of my senses?' he wondered. Lester and Angelina were crouching and scouting around in the room, trying to find a place to hide. Their mouths hung open and they looked terrified as they watched the tree slowly turning into a Beyblade. Unfortunately for them, they couldn't find a place to hide, and were unable to cope up with what was happening around them. Then, in panic, not knowing what to do, they huddled together in a corner of the room, screaming, so loud that Alex had to shout over their voices, 'LOWER YOUR VOICE!'

When the wolves opened their mouths, the trio noticed extremely smelly, decayed, deep-brown teeth. It seemed as if the odd sight of the teeth gave Lester and Angelina the willies and they closed their eyes out of fear, huddling more tightly as if they were going to break through the corner of the wall any moment.

Alex stood there, admiring the toughness of that evil creature, not even flinching when he saw their mouths. He stood still and upright. This was one of his remarkable qualities—to uphold courage and faith in himself. Then, to his amazement, the large pointed teeth of the wolves started growing at a very fast pace, becoming longer and at last curving at the ends, such that all the teeth stuck out of their large, scaly, ugly black mouths like horizontal daggers fixed on a large brown-coloured Beyblade.

The spiky Beyblade started to spin, faster than anything Alex had seen before. Lester fidgeted, sitting with his eyes shut tightly. Then the Beyblade started charging towards the only moving thing in the room—Alex. He shuddered and watched it draw closer and closer. He started jogging backwards, keeping an eye on that deadly beast. He soon found himself taking the support of the wall, trying to maintain a distance from the beast. The killer Multiwolf showed no signs of stopping. It was going to smack into Alex.

Though disheartened and helpless, Alex suddenly got an idea. 'Let it come closer; I'll move at the eleventh hour and let it smash into the wall,' he plotted instantly. The creature moved nearer, bit by bit...

SMACK! *Drrrrr...*

It ran into the metal mesh-covered wall, as Alex moved away at the very last moment. The Beyblade's long pointed teeth broke and became blunt as they brushed along the walls' metal mesh. Finally, the entire teeth broke and fell into pieces. The Multiwolf screamed and was hauled to the ground. To Alex's relief, it vanished with a *pop*.

'That, sir,' Lester spoke up, 'was good riddance.'

Suddenly, a familiar voice echoed in the room, drowning out the sound of Lester's compliment. Apparently, it was only heard by Alex, as his friends' faces showed no sign of being aware of any noise. 'Congratulations, you have managed to get through the first two tasks,' it said and a badge appeared on Alex's chest.

The First Two Tasks

This was so shocking and relieving at the same time that Alex let out a huge 'Whoa!'

The incident left him exhausted. He woke up feeling drowsy, with his heart beating out of his chest. He then woke Lester and Angelina up from their imagined nightmares and told them what transpired a while back. They were surprised to know the sequence of events. Then they ate some fruits, took a few gulps of water and though they were in a smelly and weary state, they slept peacefully on the floor. But Lester was awake, blinking rapidly as he lay next to Alex.

'Do you still believe that the challenges exist?' Lester asked Alex, as Angelina snored next to him.

'You mean to say you don't?'

'N-No... I truly wish that whatever that man had said was fake. But... there seems to be some sense in all this and the series of incidences point towards something else. We had the first challenge, the ghoul experience. Then there were stairs leading to the second one, I guess the one we are in...' Pointing towards another direction he continued, '... You see, there's a shutter door in this room, which might get us to the third challenge... and there could be ten such doors in all...each leading to the next challenge... At least that's what I think... Ain't I right, Alex?'

'Mm hmm. Let's check out the third challenge tomorrow. That will perhaps convince us that these challenges are genuine.'

'Yeah, we had a rough day today And what's with that badge? How did you get it?.'

'It was nothing much. I heard this voice congratulating me for getting through the first two challenges and then this badge appeared on my shirt... Seems like some kind of magic rewards you with these stupid badges. I guess we're in for more to come rolling in.'

The First Two Tasks

'What do you mean? More magic's gonna come to us?'

'I was talking about the badges, Lester.'

'Oh. And, by the way, I'm feeling kinda... exhausted. I'm just gonna get some sleep. Goodnight, bro,' Lester said at last as he lay down on the floor and closed his eyes.

'Good night.' replied Alex, starting to get lost in his own thoughts.

Sometime later, it turned out that only Lester and Angelina were asleep, as Alex was busy wondering while he lay on the cold floor, 'What's all this...? It's unbelievable. Plane crash, killer whale, wandering around, chased by animals, "Cavernal Mess", the man with the *forever living potion*, two challenges, Beyblade and badge...I...we... can't even contact our parents for help. They must be worried about us. Would we get any aid? Where are we heading towards? Is there more disaster to follow?' he thought, with the questions running through his mind like a merry-go-round.

Then, he glanced at Lester and Angelina and saw that they were asleep. 'Idea! Let's sleep!' he murmured to himself and slept on the cold floor, shivering.

The second day was far more disastrous than the first. This was their condition in the beginning, and no one knew what life and fate had for them in their, of course, DISASTROUS future.

\..\... `'

Chapter 8

The Helpful Dream and 'Beauties First!'

Alex witnessed a really terrible dream. It scared the guts out of him, making him wake up with a start. He was badly tempted to scream as he lay on the floor, but he couldn't. It was as if he had lost his voice for a while.

He and his friends started lifting the shutter of the door—this was the entrance to the third challenge. The three of them used all of their energy to lift it up and found themselves in a dark room, though it was not as dark as the one in the second challenge. Two old-fashioned lamps burned in the middle of the room. There was a door on the opposite wall, and separating Alex and his friends from it was a large pit.

Alex could sense the presence of evil energies and creepiness down that pit. He heard splashing of water from below. 'Just swimming, hah!' he exclaimed to himself, ignoring his detections. They moved further without being aware of what lay ahead. Incidentally, all of them abruptly fell down, followed by a *SPLASH*. Soon, Alex found himself shivering in the cold water of the pit.

He felt something sharp, pierce his buttocks. To his surprise, the whole room lit up, as two more lamps on each side of the already lit lamps started burning. The new lamps weren't noticeable earlier. He heard the screams of Lester and Angelina, and subsequently turned his head around to scan the surroundings. He saw his friends' fleshy bodies ripped to skeletons by... by... PIRANHAS. 'First killer whale, now piranhas... My friends are *dead*... No... it can't be,' sobbed Alex. Obviously, he didn't realize that this was a dream, and the incident appeared real to him.

Just then, a piranha pounced upon his throat and he felt a sharp pain.

He woke up, shivering with cold and fear. His wristwatch showed 9:00 a.m. While trying to analyse the purpose of his dream, he thought, 'Was this the

The Helpful Dream and 'Beauties First!'

third task? If so, we ought to be very cautious. I'll *not* let my friends die. I'll need to look for useful equipment when we reach there.' He woke up his friends and described his dream. Thereafter, he shared his thoughts, apprehensions and the possibilities. At last, when he was done, he added, 'Please, I request you both to be cautious and prepared.'

Alex set off with his scared but eager friends, nervously thinking about what'll happen next... Will they be torn apart or will they survive? Alex pushed the door open. The room was the same one as in his dream—two lit lamps in the middle, pit, door, hidden lamps, evil energies, splashing of water.

He created a fire with wood and flint rocks scattered around him. Then, he took a long burning stick and held it in his hand with a firm grip. Lester and Angelina seemingly remembered Alex's warnings, so they didn't move towards their deaths in the pit. All they did was to stand there in attention position, not moving a bit. Alex quickly tossed up the burning wooden stick in the air above the centre of the pit. Its light revealed a suspended rope, before the stick fell into the water-filled, piranha-infested black chasm.

It was a rope made up of several long noodle-like branches. But, Alex was unable to assess their strength. 'Swing through the rope and get through,' Alex planned. But, this could be put to work only if the rope was strong enough. He threw some of the fire-lit wooden twigs by mere 'guess-throws' in the air, managing to entangle them into the rope. The *branch rope* was now clearly visible. He was astonished to find that the rope was metallic. 'Just swing through it and try *not* to touch any of the burning little wooden pieces. Else, you know, you'll get a second-degree burn and get eaten by piranhas. Anyway, let's try to be positive. Okay, so now, after me, you two will follow suit. At the count of three, Angelina, you'll jump. At two, Lester, you'll come. One, that's for me. We'll need to hurry as we can't let the fire extinguish because we'll swing with pressure and our movement will cause the air to stir, which will surely extinguish the burning sticks; then there'll be less light for anyone of us to have a grip on the rope. We need to hurry, because we can't let this thing get even a *little bit* of time for breaking. Okay?' said Alex, making the plan clear.

The Helpful Dream and 'Beauties First!'

'You're scaring me, dude. Couldn't you be a little easier?' asked Lester, apparently frightened. Angelina made a face like *I'm gonna die for sure.*

Now, let's start the countdown. Five... Four... Three...'

SWINNGGG!

When his friends swung, he didn't forget to continue the countdown. 'Two... One!' he shouted. Seconds later, he found himself next to his friends, his legs trembling due to the adrenaline rush and fear. Alex had literally fallen down on his knees, petrified.

They passed the challenge, which Lester had named 'The Piranha group and its sharp teeth causing death and skeleton'.

'Do you really need to be *naming* experiences like this? Are they precious?' Angelina asked.

'Um, no?'

'Then cut it out.'

The third challenge proved to be a severely terrifying task. They were at it for only two days, but experienced extremely dangerous, almost life-threatening situations.

They had so far succeeded in completing three tasks. Alex wondered how terrifying the remaining seven would be.

'What a terribly tough day I had. Believe me, if you'd been in a similar situation, you would have run away screaming (See, I'm not judging your personality, so don't be furious at me)' thought Alex, making a mental note about getting this written as ***views−judging−conversation−between−writer−and−reader*** in the book he was going to write, sharing the ordeal he went through on the island.

It certainly is a matter of fact that at this place there would be only terror, frightfulness and god-knows-what other horrible conditions for the survivors. There would be no signs of happiness here. The friends were somehow surviving at this fearful place, encouraging each other. They were seated in a huge dark room with only two yellow lamps burning inside, with the curtains and doors sealed shut. How restless would one feel if he/she were in a similar situation.

Angelina asked, 'Um...uhh...well, what now, get into another hocus-pocus?'

'Challenge,' Alex corrected.

'Yeah, whatever. Is it really the need of the hour to get killed? No way. I'd rather like to eat something first. Starving is hard.'

'Okay, then. Here you go,' replied Alex, giving her another fruit of the tree they had climbed.

They helped themselves on some fruits. Then, Alex stood up and said, 'Let's get going.' They pulled the door open, and the room where they sat became visible. To their amazement, the room looked grand and imposing, similar to one inside a maintained mansion, and unlike the one on the other side of the island. It had white tiles, royal yellow lamps and shining smooth golden walls, with a silver ceiling on top, The room was also equipped with food, such as potato chips, bread, as well as bathroom accessories, such as soaps and other toiletries. A modern bed, Wi-Fi, telephone, desks, side tables were some of the other objects in the room. On the floor was a blazing red carpet, adding a touch of royalty. Alex was delighted to see the top-class facilities. His frown changed to smile as soon as he saw the room. Angelina and Lester's eyes sparkled with joy. But when they remembered that it was part of a challenge, they turned their heads towards each other in suspicion.

'Cool. Don't think of this as a challenge. It all seems so nice... Lemme just use this notepad...' Lester said, but no one had the time to reply, as suddenly the room was filled with a strange fragrance.

'It's kinda awkward, I know. But yeah, the room smells of different flavours—cherry, tart, cakes—as well as deodorants and room fresheners,' said Alex to his friends.

'Candies, soaps and a lot more, you know, *sweet* stuff,' added Angelina.

Alex couldn't help smelling. 'At this place, awkwardness never ends,' he said to himself. But, within seconds, he guessed that this smell could be a trap, and the room itself *was* a part of the challenge. 'Really, another piece of cake?' he thought. He went towards the dressing table, grabbed a hand towel and covered his nose with it. Then he went through the mist, which had suddenly appeared out of nowhere, to find his friends. Angelina was nowhere to be seen. He saw Lester a few metres away. He went up to him and warned, 'Be cautious,' still holding his hand towel over his nose.

Lester appeared disoriented, somewhat different than usual. He replied smiling, 'But...Beauties first!' Instantaneously, he danced off in the mist, subsequently disappearing from Alex's vision. When

The Helpful Dream and 'Beauties First!'

Alex heard the word 'Beauties' he suddenly got a hint of the challenge. These 'Beauties' were hypnotizing his friends through the smell. But who were these Beauties?

At that very moment, his ears were filled with a loud screeching sound and he fell on the ground, unconscious.

Fortunately enough, he woke up in the nick of time. But perhaps it was the wrong time...or the right time to wake up, to be conscious.

It was a faint sound emanating from a distance that woke him up. He heard squealing, chattering and some awkward noises, as if some insects were buzzing and talking to each other in their own creepy language. He opened his eyes, and was shocked to see the scene in front of him. He still lay at the same place, but... now he wasn't staring at the silver ceiling, but at...

...At a dusty iron ceiling, with rocks all around it carved into dreadful figurines of dull-coloured demons, and he noticed scary and creepy ones. The ambience was paranormal.

At the sight of the ceiling, he thought, 'WHAT THE HELL! THIS PLACE IS CERTAINLY HELL!

This creepiness, oof! A trap. Now this room has divulged its true colours. Or rather, the dull colours of the demons. The place seems as old as Stone Age... Let's see, what's next.' He was a little flustered at first, but regained his composure soon, and tried his best to stay calm. He was at a dangerous place and there was no trace of his friends, or his parents, who could've helped him. He was disheartened, broken... and couldn't stay calm for long.

He wondered if those figurines were alive... But they weren't even blinking.

'Thank God for that,' thought Alex.

He got up from the cold slippery floor and noticed a tunnel leading to nowhere. Only a shade of orange and warm light emanated from inside the tunnel, while the end of the tunnel was filled with an orange mist.

He walked deeper and deeper inside it. The orange light had started to glow so brightly that Alex had to shut his eyes while walking. After pushing his way through it for about 250 metres, Alex opened his eyes to see the surroundings around him. It was a very awkward sight, and appeared to be a part of the passageway from where the glowing mist had started to vanish.

The Helpful Dream and 'Beauties First!'

At the end of passageway were the Beauties, as named by Lester and assumed by Alex. They appeared to be busy cleaning the ground. At that part of the tunnel, the glowing mist had started to dissipate. The Beauties had a woman's body, but their faces were not certain. It was either of insects or animals.

Alex's eyes drifted towards the orange mist, which was trapped in transparent boxes, about two to three hundred in number. But, it turned out to be lava. One of the Beauties was scraping and scouring out lava from a corner of the tunnel, just where the passageway ended. She had the face of a rabbit. Some had human-sized faces of mosquitoes and house flies. The insects' faces were not distinguishably visible, but the Beauties had bulging eyes embedded on their insect-like faces. They wore dresses of women, similar to one worn during a Salsa dance, but unlike Salsa outfits their dresses were white.

Alex crouched in the passageway and moved aside, hiding from the Beauties, to observe the place. He found that the tunnel was bordered with ball-like igneous rocks. The Beauties were carrying out various activities, which Alex was unable to comprehend. For instance, there was one who beat an iron rod with her hand, such that the rod was bending at a certain angle. 'Gotta be careful. These insects look creepy, stupid, but strong,' Alex thought.

In another corner of the place, Lester and Angelina were hanged upside down by a rope, bound around their feet. It was attached to a pulley system. On the other side of the rope, a large and heavy stone was tied as weight. Both of them hung unconscious, their eyes closed. Beneath them was a large cauldron filled with boiling green liquid, which Alex suspected to be dangerous.

'They can be tipped into that green liquid any time soon. Needa save them,' he thought.

He looked up and saw that the wall made up of igneous rocks. In the centre of the wall was a circular opening through which sunlight entered the place. When Alex saw this, he immediately realized that they were inside a volcano, whose lava had been sucked out by the Beauties and stored in boxes. Their nature was such that they would prey on anyone who barged into their territory. 'They might not have *killed* my friends. But, they might've planned to lure me into a trap, when I came looking for them... I see. They're *too* vigilant,' Alex observed.

The Helpful Dream and 'Beauties First!'

Thinking about the critical state of his friends, Alex decided that he would fight the Beauties to save his friends. But as he took his first step in the camp of enemies, his thought process changed. He instantaneously stopped from proceeding and thought, 'No, if I go like this, I may put myself in danger, too. And *yeow*, I don't wanna get hanged upside down; and that way made to vomit. I must think of a strategy,' and he was lost deep in thought.

He knew he had to hurry. 'But, safety for all three of us is my prime concern.'

He started plotting his intrusion for some time, in between glancing back towards his friends to ensure they weren't tipped into the cauldron with the green liquid.

At last he came with a plan. Though it was very risky, he thought, 'I have to do everything instantaneously without giving anyone much time. Lemme run into their camp, get hold of my friends, knock out one of the boxes and soar with a *blast* of lava.'

So he ran off in the midst of the Beauties. He could not see the expression of shock on their insect-faces but could merely *guess* their surprise as he ran through them at an awfully fast speed. He then quickly grabbed his friends by the waist, pulled them in such a way that the rope snapped free and then tipped over the nearest box full of lava with his leg.

BLAST!

As the lava drained out of the box and touched the warm floor, it brushed past the other boxes of lava, and hit the rocks placed inside the tunnel, somehow reacting and leading to an explosion. Literally, a **volcano explosion**, not a *volcanic eruption*.

The Beauties, circular igneous rocks, lava, large chunks from the surface of the volcano were flying high in the sky. In the midst of this chaos, Alex had a firm grip on his friends' waists and soared fast into the sky. He looked down, but everything was a blur.

Suddenly, a circular igneous rock came hurtling out of nowhere and hit his hand, so hard that he had to withdraw his grip on Angelina's waist. As he became aware of his pain, he saw an unconscious Angelina falling towards the ground speedily.

'Angelina! No!' a grief-struck Alex yelled in shock and pain. The sudden burst of his vocal cord woke up Lester. 'W-What's...happened...Angelina?' he started murmuring. Alex was traumatized and wished

The Helpful Dream and 'Beauties First!'

to calm down a little. He tried hard to keep his hope alive for her, but Angelina's plight preoccupied his mind.

As he was absorbed in his thoughts, he did not realize that he and Lester were falling down towards the ground at a great speed. He felt the pressure of air whirring past his body, and soon found himself very close to the ground: a rocky terrain with red soil.

He closed his eyes, ready to face the danger and pain. To his amazement, he bumped onto something soft and slimy, which he suspected to be one of the Beauties, and bounced off from the ground. Before he knew it, his head hit a rock and his vision went black, and eventually he was knocked unconsciousness.

Chapter 9

Life's Gloomy

| Florida |

'Dear, I gotta hurry. Pack the essentials. And I need it done *quick*,' said Eric to his wife Isabella, as he rushed out of the house to join the rest of the lot. They hurriedly moved towards the Army Airport in Clive's Mercedes.

After the security check, they seated themselves in the waiting area.

The flight was delayed due to snowfall. Deeply tensed and apprehensive of what lay ahead, the group found it extremely difficult to kill time.

They sat there, worried. After about six hours, Eric checked his watch. It was 4:30 p.m. He peeped out of the window of the waiting area. The snowfall had stopped. But the runway still had a thick layer of snow on it. The Army had just started cleaning it with hi-tech machines.

He looked at Clive and Clinton and found them to be talking to each other regarding the whereabouts of their children. They were informed that they would be taking off for Wasor Island in another half an hour. He rested his head on the chair's headrest and closed his eyes, trying to relax himself.

| Wasor |

Sometime later, Alex woke up, but with some difficulty. He opened his eyes, only to gaze at the orange sky at dawn?

'No. Not like this,' he thought. He had been through a lot and he had lost Angelina. He realized that he had to wake up; he could not end like that. He had to get up... He *had* to get up... He had to...

He gathered courage and convinced his mind and body to get up, but it wasn't easy. He tried to lift his hand but it hurt badly. He tried again and again but to no avail.

He groped around in the red, dirty soil for some support. He felt something cold, rough and slippery under his hand. It was the black rock that his head had hit upon.

Though in ineffable pain, he lifted himself up taking support of the same rock, his unconscious doer. He looked around. The scene was unusual. He and Lester were surrounded on either side by a very dense and dark forest. Upwards in the sky, dirt was flying all over due to the blast.

'Blast,' he remembered, and with this he was reminded of Angelina. Tears welled up in his eyes. He had lost her.

'What have I not lost?' he thought. 'Precisely, almost everything. Angelina...' he recalled, and sighed wearily aching with pain, both physically and emotionally. 'Lester is still not fully conscious, parents are worried about us and even my limbs are badly hurt. And...and what have I got? Only shock, grief and pain. It seems like getting crushed under a pile of stone boulders...'

He couldn't stop himself from wondering why was he even destined to be on this island. Each time he had got into trouble, he had cursed destiny. 'I want this *destiny* to get under me. I wish I could change it. It... it's really annoying...'

Trying to calm himself down, he recalled that he had once read in a spiritual magazine that whatever happens in life happens for a purpose.

'But what *is* the purpose...?' he was unable to get any answer.

His situation made him lose hope. He shivered at the thought of the future, which looked uncertain and gloomy. He had always thought of destiny as a superpower, as a messiah for those who are in difficult situations. His destiny had always brought laurels to him and he had always been optimistic to tide over difficult times.

But then, here destiny was failing him. Alex, along with Lester, had suffered bad luck. 'Its purpose *had* to be negative... That's what I've figured out now. Are the remaining tasks also gonna be like this...? Or more ghastly...? I'm afraid we'll die... Alas, it's destiny...' he thought in despair.

Alex saw an unconscious Lester some feet away, with his backpack still flung over his shoulders. He was lying on the ground as if he were a corpse.

'I hope he is alive,' Alex said to himself.

He tried to get to him by walking, but the excruciating pain didn't allow him to do so. He managed to reach him somehow, crawling like an animal, on four legs.

He knew that he must gain some energy to help him able to stand. As he took out an apple from the bag, a familiar voice bouncing off the dark trees echoed around him.

It was the voice he had heard after completing the first two tasks. He then recognized it as Vishwaroopaha's.

'Well done, boy! You are very clever. I'm impressed! Now as a reward, have this,' it said, and another badge fitted itself on Alex's shirt.

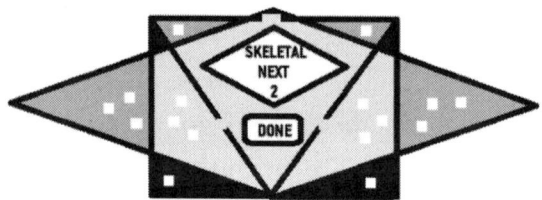

'Huh, I'm so badly injured and already lost my dear friend...,' he thought, disheartened by the turn of events. '... and this old man is saying that I have done well? What *is* well here, by the way...?'

But, realizing that he had cleared two challenges and reached a new one, he said to himself, 'I must not even *think* in a tone like that. I've actually received a reward. Reward...?' He speculated curiously, 'Do these badges have any relation to me or the challenges...? Or... are they just a proof of my success?'

'Never mind,' he muttered to himself.

He was in a mixed state of hope and despair, and wondered whether he was brave enough to be rewarded. At the time, he wasn't aware that he were to receive more badges in the coming days.

'But... how is this metal badge a reward?'

In a desperate attempt, he ran his fingers over the badge and suddenly felt a surge of strength. His pain subsided immediately.

'Whoa! This was the reward to strengthen me!' he discovered.

He stood up, amazed. He tried to wake Lester up and tell him what had just transpired. He put the apple back inside the backpack and zipped it up.

'How do I wake this man up...? He seems deeply hurt. It's likely that nothing will happen if I splash water on his face or try to move him a little. What do I do...?' he thought, regardless of the fact that there was a chance that Lester might not even be alive.

Then he noticed another badge on Lester's dirt-coated shirt. It said "Survivor". A ray of hope gleamed in Alex's eyes. He took Lester's hand hurriedly and made it touch the badge, hoping it would have the same effect on him. But nothing happened. Neither did he open his eyes nor did he utter any sound... Lester just lay there, motionless as before. Alex was in despair again.

However, soon he got over it. He still suspected that his friend's cure was related to that badge. He thought about it again and again. After ruminating for an extremely long time, such that it was semi-dark (in his surroundings as well as in his mind), he finally settled on an investigation.

'First of all, let's do this,' he muttered to himself.

Anxiously, he unhooked Lester's badge from his shirt, and observed it carefully, trying to search for clues. He held the badge up in the air with his right hand. What he saw was astonishing.

Rays of yellow light appeared to be emerging out of the badge. In no time, he found that the yellow rays were connecting the badge to a yellow light in the bushes. Concentrating and observing carefully, he saw that these were irregularly shaped yellowish orange glowing spots in the bushes. The bushes were in front of the dark canopy of trees. He was awestruck.

'Wha–the hell!' he exclaimed after observing the strange process. His face looked like a policeman conducting a raid, who had found meat instead of black money, at a place where he had expected to find a huge amount.

'Huh, I knew some weird activity would happen now, as it always does on this island,' he thought. Then something clicked within him. He crouched down and slowly reached the bushes where the yellow spots glowed. He was still holding the badge in air, trying not to break the ray's contact with the spots, which helped him reach the exact area where the orange-yellow light glowed in the bushes.

He touched one of the irregularly shaped yellow light, and found them to be a slimy, sticky, but warm, substance.

'Warm? In such a cold weather... No way!' thought Alex.

He pulled out one of those substances from the bushes. When not seen in the connecting light of the badge, they appeared to be a blackish green and brown substance, which looked and smelt like pig sludge.

'Yuck.' Alex first thought that he must throw this disgusting thing away. But then he remembered that he had to cure Lester.

He made Lester come in contact with the substance, making him touch it with his hands. He then touched it to Lester's lips, hoping that Lester would spring up and eat that thing, saying, 'Dish ish reeully tashty, bro.'

But nothing happened.

Thinking, 'For Lester's sake, I need to do this,' Alex did something awful.

He *fed* it to Lester.

'After all, it looks like it grew in those bushes. It must be natural. The badge has only indicated its presence. Natural things, unless poisonous, don't harm anyone. But, I hope they do cure...' Alex reasoned before committing the act.

And at last, Lester opened his eyes.

'Wha... what happened?' he said softly, starting to sit upright on the rocky red soil.

Alex was relieved. His efforts had paid off! He told him everything that took place while he was unconscious, including losing Angelina.

After getting to know about Angelina, Lester's facial expressions changed dramatically, as if all of sudden he had turned from a movie star to a penniless destitute who had recently found out that not only him, but his entire family's fortune, had been wiped out.

Trying to get over Angelina's loss, he told Alex what had happened with him.

He said, 'Huh, when that smell hypnotized me, I dreamt of...' he stopped abruptly thinking for a moment, his face puzzled and scared.

He continued, 'Um...tempting things. As soon as I came back to my senses, I found myself hanging upside down with my head just above a cauldron with boiling-hot green liquid. When the liquid's smell reached my nose, I fell unconscious... And you know what happened to me after that.'

'Mmm...okay...all this is happening because of me. Neither of this would have happened if I had not accepted this rally of challenges. All because of me...' Alex said as tears welled up in his eyes. Lester tried to sympathize with him but Alex was dejected. He was slowly losing courage and hope.

'Um...true, I guess you should not have taken up those challenges. But, let's look ahead. What should we do now?' Lester said in an informal tone.

Alex burst out on hearing this.

'You...you... HERE I AM BADLY GRIEVING AND YOU ARE JUST...' he shouted angrily, but lowered his voice at last.

This was the first time in his life that he had lost patience and was about to say something bad to Lester. Never in the past had he spoken abusively to his friend.

Lester was shocked and startled by the look on his face, but he didn't reply and instead turned his face in another direction, quietly thinking something. Alex was surprised. He was expecting Lester to fight back, using the same language that he did. This would have surely led to a quarrel. But Lester had figured out that this wasn't the main subject to focus on. What was important was to keep Alex calm. Alex patiently thought about Lester's words and realized that he wasn't wrong in what he said. He didn't mean to hurt Alex, but was trying to help him find a way out of the mess they were in.

But it did not make Alex's mood better. The only way to keep him at his normal behaviour was to make him understand that he should not blame himself for the current situation.

Lester said apprehensively, 'Please, I...' he stopped for a moment, as if he didn't have words to express himself.

Alex cut him off, patted him on the back in a friendly manner, saying, 'Sorry for that outburst. I just blew my temper meter off...heh!'

'Yes... We'll stay strong. We are best friends... Aren't we?'

'Yeah. We will remain friends forever and we shall definitely stay strong,' Alex said as he smiled.

But Alex couldn't breathe easy. Stretched before him were a trail of obstacles. He could not be at peace due to the turmoil brewing inside him, thinking of what lay ahead. To relax his mind, he told Lester that they should go to bed and get some sleep. Of course, there was no bed there and they had to lie down on the rocky red soil, resolving to deal with the future plans the next morning.

The stones' sharp tips were piercing their backs. Ignoring the pain, Alex recorded in his mind, 'Three days, two nights, huh... Is this all gonna lead us... or especially me into hell? I got my friends into this mess and now Angelina is no more...' he sobbed, but continued thinking, 'She's... she's... d-e-a-d... No. This can't be true. She's alright, I believe,' he thought, at last lighting up a little candle of hope.

He felt bad for himself and everyone—all three of them. He then thought of the consequences. 'If I hadn't been so "kind" to these animals... and hadn't accepted all these arduous tasks, none of this would've ever happened. We would have been in a better condition. We would have somehow survived much easily than we are doing now. We would've sought help and would've been at home at this very minute,' thinking this, he felt extremely sorry and guilty.

Chapter 10

The 'Almost Dead' Experience

As dawn lined the horizon in faint yellow, Alex woke up and thought, 'Another day full of stress, with bad things lying in wait for us.'

His surroundings were quite bad. Creepy-crawlies and mosquitoes were closing in on both of them. His comrade, who lay beside him, was snoring badly, as if he had never slept before. The sun's bright light and the smell emanating from the Beauties' dead bodies made the situation worse. Alex decided to get ready for the 'All-in-one-bad-happenings' day. He set out to demolish his friend's 'act of hibernation'. Alex quite liked the nickname he had chosen for Lester's deep slumber.

When woken up by Alex, Lester looked at him irritatingly. 'Why did you do this?' his eyes seemed to convey. Alex reminded him, 'Whoa there, guy! Don't make a face like that. You're on a strange island in the middle of the Atlantic Ocean and not in your cosy bedroom.'

This seemed to shake him up unexpectedly. 'He can get a little peculiar sometimes,' Alex thought, seeing Lester's sudden change of facial expressions, from loathing to being vigilant.

'Let's get going,' said Lester.

'But where?'

'Um...to that abstract dusty gate over there,' Lester pointed towards a rectangular shutter gate, which was yellow in colour with black stripes around the edges.

'Things are just... annoying and disturbing. The so-called abstract gate described by Lester signals the advent of bad things,' Alex wished he could somehow transform these into something pleasant at that very instant. Suddenly, he yearned to enjoy the latest movie in the theatre.

'But...alas. Fate. Why is it so powerful? And... and... why can't I change it? One day, I promise myself, I'll find a way to conquer it,' thought Alex as he crumbled hopelessly while making that unattainable vow.

The 'Almost Dead' Experience

Gathering strength, he thought, *Adventure awaits*. Whenever he was in Florida City, the same idea made him think of a stupid family magazine with the theme of *Outing*. But at that point of time, it seemed like the cover page of a horror book, titled *Alex Drake's Death*.

'I am moving towards my death...isn't it?' he thought. But his *brainy* antivirus system said, 'Nah. You got through four challenges and survived. What'll you get by dying now?'

'You have a point,' Alex said to himself.

Alex cleared his mind and focused on Lester, who was moving like a drunken person. 'What a magical thing is this...drowsiness,' Alex thought.

'Have this. You'll get some strength,' he advised Lester, handing him a dusty apple. He ate it voraciously, not caring to take the dust off it.

Weak and injured, they took more than double the time required to reach the nearby gate. Alex imagined that their speed was like two drowsy men walking in a super-slo-mo video.

The next difficulty—how to open this gate? Their concern however was unwarranted. As they reached closer to the gate, it automatically opened with a loud *krrr* sound.

In front of them was a huge, but dilapidated, ancient building. Inside was a dimly lit rectangular room made up of copper walls of different shades, which in turn were inscribed with Stone Age pictographic warnings. There was a basic wooden door at the far end of the room. Bits of stones and rubble littered the floor.

'Shhhhhhhh,' a windy sound echoed inside. When the two of them entered the room, the walls became darker, as the shutter door behind them slid down automatically and trapped the two.

'What kind of a challenge is this? Do we have to do an archaeologist's job? Or is this just a technique to drift us into sleep and kill us in our dreams?' Lester said.

'For once, your guess seems right.'

'What do you mean by *for once?*' Lester asked, eyeing him like a wolf.

'Um...nothing. Let's move on.'

All of a sudden, the bits of stones and rubble lying on the floor collected together and solidified into stone warriors, whose attire resembled the Crusaders of Christianity.

'They are five in number, made of stone, from *underwear* to the *cranium*. Hmm... don't mind, bro.

The 'Almost Dead' Experience

I-I... j-just want to be humorous sometimes to keep the mood up,' Lester tried to speak cheerfully, but his voice cracked in between because of the sight of the warriors.

The stone warriors had a stern look on their badly carved faces. Just looking into their eyes made Alex feel like belching out the whole can of 'crunchies' he had eaten sometime back, and he felt like cursing the day Lester had invited him to this deadly... *whatever*.

All of a sudden, the stone warriors started to move in perfect formation of five towards the darkest wall of the room and leaned on the wall using their hands as support.

Lester said, 'What the heck are you all doing, fellas?'

'I don't think they're too chatty,' Alex replied.

'*Yer* right, captain.'

Soon, their purpose of leaning against the wall became clear. Some of the copper from the wall collected on their hands and turned into swords.

From nowhere, Vishwaroopaha's serious voice started to bob in Alex's head. It said, 'The fifth challenge—the stone soldiers with their copper swords.'

'In for another blood-curling task,' Alex said, with the last word being obstructed by an angry sigh. It came out of his mouth like 'tghusssk'. He pledged not to waste time naming the challenges, unless Vishwaroopaha did so in Alex's mind. He knew that the upcoming challenges would be much harder, and that meant lesser time to think of a terrifying name. And would he really remember the names? Even if he did, who would ever listen to them?

'This island seems to take full advantage of us being here, especially this series of harrowing tasks,' Lester said, distracting Alex from his bizarre thoughts.

'This time, "*Yer* right, captain",' said Alex, copying Lester's funny style.

Being with him for a considerable time, Alex had learnt to be cheerful in adverse situations. An old memory came whizzing in his mind, the time when the two had got into serious trouble.

The incident was stored in his computer-like brain with the file name as MSTFRSTRATINMOMNT. Whenever this experience popped up in his mind, he felt aggressive and wanted to throw whatever he had in his hand. But one day he assured himself, 'Nah, that's not me. I am not destructive. Need to get over it.'

You get the idea.

The 'Almost Dead' Experience

On his tenth birthday, which fell during school vacations, his mother had asked him to celebrate the occasion at his football academy, saying he would have a good time with his friends on his birthday. He found it to be a fair deal. 'But on one condition. I wanna take Lester with me as my companion,' he said.

'Okay, I agree,' replied his mother, laughing at Alex's innocence.

Alex instinctively remembered the day, as he and Lester moved cheerfully on the streets, listening to Lester's favourite song 'For he's a jolly good fellow'. It was a sight to see. That day, even the Sun seemed to be singing along with them. 'Anybody who would have watched us that day would have envied our friendship. *Wow! How calm, classical, jovial, enriching...* It was a wonderful evening, with the two of us walking cheerfully towards the academy...' Alex recalled the happy moment.

When he and Lester entered the football academy and moved towards the field, the scene was quite unusual. Little children, with an average age of 7, were playing their kiddie football game. Soon Alex realized his fault and smacked his head with his hand funnily. They had mistakenly entered the kids' field. Without wasting time, they turned and headed towards their field. They were carefree and walked with confidence.

But soon it became clear that their cheerful mood was to no avail. Alex was destined to have bad fate on his birthday. When he entered the field, Peter Colter, his archenemy, stared at him with a furious look on his face. He was around three years older than Alex, and was the only guy in the academy with whom Alex was not on good terms. Alex tried to escape his gaze, but it did not help matters. Peter came nearer, accompanied by a few hooligans. Although Alex had a good friend circle, none of them were present there to support him in that moment.

Peter, along with his cronies, approached Alex and Lester arrogantly, a football rolling between his legs. 'Examinations over?'

'Yeah. It's my birthday. See, I got some chocol–'
BASH

Soon, the knocked down Alex had a bloody nose, eyes bloodshot, a flattened and puffy red face with a fused expression of anger and sadness.

Lester barely saw all this as he had already been dragged away from that spot before Peter had hit Alex.

The 'Almost Dead' Experience

He was also made to fall to the other merciless and ruthless figures.

After sometime, Alex and Lester emerged out of the field, shocked and terrified. Despite trying his best, Alex couldn't forget the scene when both of them were crying and reporting to each other about what had happened to them while calling those brats names. He didn't know why those boys tried to harm him on his special day.

He didn't remember what had happened afterwards; neither did he talk about it with Lester.

Unknowingly, relating the current situation to old memories, Alex noticed the group of deadly stone troops charging towards them. With fierce expressions on their faces, they moved slowly towards Alex and Lester. Alex tried to think of an effective plan to make the soldiers back off.

Lester said, 'Some rock destroyer, or even a chainsaw would have worked here. Have any?'

'Nah. Don't think so.'

'Then spiked shoes may work.' Lester took out a few metal spikes, attached to a leather piece and kept in a plastic box, from his backpack. The spikes allowed him to stick the leather to the sole of one of his shoes. 'Brought these just in case...'

'Needa clap. But...'

Suddenly, a stone soldier crumbled to tiny pieces. It was Lester who had hit him. He now had a crooked smile on his face but was left with only one shoe, that on his left foot.

'Right is always right,' said Lester cunningly.

The other four soldiers seemed undaunted by this and continued their work of wading through the air towards the *rock demolisher* Lester.

But the warriors' act of being unfazed was recognized as a fair thought by Alex.

'These warriors are just like, *"Why to stop yourself from going on an exhilarating trip, when you know that despite being hit by a wagon your friend will join you soon?"* Alex thought.

His doubt wasn't wrong at all. The warrior soon repaired and reconstituted itself, and became the way it was before being wrecked badly.

Alex, now seriously amazed, said, 'Spikes wasted. Game over.'

Chapter 11
DarkService

'Difficult situation. This is an unbreakable wall,' Lester said in a hurry, dodging a copper blade from one of the soldiers.

'There is no way we can counter-attack. We need to plan meticulously to defeat them,' replied Alex, disheartened, dodging another copper sword. His voice unintentionally attracted more troops. He now had four of those five swords pointing towards him.

Running away from them, while not breaking the *face-to-face* contact, he got pushed and was pinned to one of the copper walls. The soldiers surrounded him in a semi-circle. He looked around, tensed, with his back towards the wall. He was girdled on all sides. He suddenly fell down and lay in the corner of the wall.

It further added to his unreal screenplay, which was unbelievable, dream-like and difficult to describe. It made him feel mad and edgy. 'Extraordinary feelings for extraordinary times, especially when one is not given time to get his last wishes fulfilled,' thought Alex. 'Without getting any opportunity, just in a fraction of time, a person can find it hard to overcome his problems. In such a situation escape is difficult. Yet, miracles do happen,' he agreed with himself. 'But here, in such a supernatural situation, there must be some miraculous incident to save us. Science, at this kind of place... impossible,' he thought.

This time his speculation didn't turn out to be right. A truly scientific wonder was executed by Lester.

Alex got this straight, even though it was really confusing. *When?*, *What?* and *Who?* were the main questions popping up in his mind right then, instead of *How?*, *Hell!* and *Hey!*, when he saw the bunch of rocky morons disintegrate rapidly, one by one, into grainy particles, not teeny-weeny chunks of rocks. Their granular demolition started from their hands, which gripped the hilts of their copper swords. In not more than 30 seconds, all the stone warriors were crushed, revealing a bright and breezy Lester with a *We did it* expression on his face. Alex saw him looking over with jokey eyes, holding a sparkling electrical wire in his hand.

Lester helped Alex get to his feet.

'Bro, how did you...? And... and from where did you get this *sparkling life saver?*' a bewildered Alex asked.

'I mean how could you actually do it? It needed perfect planning and timing, and you didn't have much time either,' Alex continued.

'I certainly don't have any magical powers to enable me to do so, nor have I acquired any on this island. I just saw the wire dangling from the door leading to the next challenge, and knowing that copper is a good conductor of electricity, I intuitively picked it up and touched it to the warriors' swords. First, I destroyed the stone warriors and then came up to save you. But I dunno how the electricity in the swords made the stone soldiers crumble to dust. Some miracle?' said Lester, triumphantly, then adding, 'For now, let's move on to the next tas–'

The door to the next challenge opened up by itself, at the mention of the work "task". Or was it something else? The entrance revealed nothing but darkness, which engulfed everything—the surroundings, the sky and even the ground.

Alex took a huge gulp of air. Lester fainted.

'Uh, not again,' Alex muttered.

There was no option but to get in.

Alex wondered 'How the hell on *this* island... Electric sparks... How could electricity be here...? But, yeah, that could be the cursed magic.'

With utmost difficulty, he carried Lester towards the dark door. 'Carrying such a flabby 200-pound boy is no easy job,' he said to himself.

Helpless, Alex thought he would rather prefer to be a creepy wizard, doing all sorts of ghastly actions in some anonymous strange world rather than carrying his friend towards another kill-off.

It took almost all of Alex's strength to carry Lester. Though unwillingly, he was forced to literally drag Lester across the floor, after giving up all hope of holding him up. Alex felt that even the word darkness could not describe his current surroundings effectively. He knew this was not mere darkness, but something more. Something that couldn't be thought, guessed or even described. It was to be felt. This time, there was no gurgling and splashing water, no acidic or attractive smell, no mansion, no creepiness, nothing. And unusually, the surroundings were so normal. 'Yet, it is blank like a plain paper, clean and white in colour...'

'Wait a minute. Did I just say white? It is actually dark and black around here. That's how weird and paranormal this island is. It has made me say the wrong things,' said Alex to himself.

'"Destructive happenings" and "Almost dead" experiences—are these two mandatory here? Work and work, huh... Are these dangers gonna get over some day? They're killing me from inside. It seems like my soul is shrieking out of fear. Rather than witnessing all this stuff, I'd love to be lost in endless space!' Alex shouted out loud.

'I'm really annoyed...' he had just started to mutter again before he was interrupted by the familiar voice of Vishwaroopaha's emanating from the sky.

'If he's so magical, then can't he himself free these animals from their curse? There's something fishy about this man. He always sends his clever words but never shows up.'

'Child, you are great. That wish of yours which you had yelled may be fulfilled one day, I promise.

I have no words for you. I want to come to you, to embrace and thank you. But alas, I am stuck here, in this mansion, where you had stayed for a while,' Vishwaroopaha said.

'Hey, can this man read my mind? In his defence, he now says that he wants to come here but can't. Another lie. And that wish... what wish... space?' Alex went blank thinking about Vishwaroopaha's words.

Suddenly, rainbow-coloured bars appeared in the air, moving up and down like voice pitch-sensing amplitude waves, in a square grid-like boundary-less darkness.

He continued, 'Do you like bright colours in darkness? What a sight to see, really. Okay, for now, let's wave off other matters. As you have got through half of the bewitched tasks, you'll get prizes. First is a remedy to cure your friend. Just wake him up. He's actually deep asleep. Second, the shock and grief you felt after losing Angelina is going to disappear now. Just listen carefully to what I have to say. She's currently making her way through a series of trials, especially designed for her to bring her back to life. She'll meet you in the second last challenge, in case you reach there... alive. Meanwhile, enjoy the time of your life in darkness. All the services of the universe are available to you for the next 15 minutes. Just say and it's done. Remember, after these 15 minutes have passed, this *DarkService* sixty-four-dimensional room will dissolve, and you and your friend will be thrown into hell. And, ah, there's a plus point too. The next task of yours is a refreshment challenge. That dangling electrical wire in the previous challenge had its source there. If you are excited to rush to the next challenge before your 15 minutes have passed, remember: Just ask the darkness. Oh... just noticed that I've wasted a lot of your time. Seriously, I need to abide by the laws of time. Only 10 minutes are left. Hurry!' his voice faded, leaving nothing but an echo of his relieving lecture's last word.

Alex was stunned, unable to speak, think, or even stand on the unnoticeable dark floor. This man always surprised him. Vishwaroopaha had helped him a lot, just in exchange for a rescue from the streets of a peculiar animal town.

To get full advantage of the minutes left, he woke Lester up and quickly gave him a brief of Vishwaroopaha's speech. Then, to test the phenomenon, he hurriedly called out aloud, 'Two large hamburgers, long curly fries and two diet cokes, please.' Suddenly a spotlight shone out of nowhere on a table appearing out of umm... nowhere. On it were the items requested by Alex. Both of them ate heartily.

'Yo, bro. Have you just started a burger company on this island? I like this stuff. By the way, I wanna be your company's manager,' Lester said humorously, apparently delighted.

Alex called out aloud again, 'I request two fully charged cell phones with video-calling facility.'

The latest models launched by a renowned company appeared on the table, and soon a superior-quality video-calling app opened on its own.

A few seconds later, Lester interrupted, stuffing himself with the last handful of fries, 'Bukhoom goo yoo wanga coll wikh gek aepp? Angelina hash no phone.'

'First of all, do not talk while stuffing your mouth. Second, our parents might be worried for us. And we're gonna contact them. We're fortunate that this time the phone is able to catch the network. From where, I... I guess that's magical, too.'

'Mmm... right.'

Alex dialled his mother's number. She accepted the call quickly, and Alex hurriedly told her about their current situation. He did not get into any kind of "Bye mom" or "Love you mom" kind of business. He told her in brief about the island, and Angelina too. He pleaded her to rescue them as soon as possible while warning her of the animals and weird surroundings. With "Good luck" exchanges, Alex hung up the call. He called out aloud, 'How much time is left?'

The countdown timer displayed 30 seconds in the black, dark air.

Alex said, 'Get us to the next challenge.'

With a blink of an eye, they were sent to a place that comprised many glass-walled rooms arranged in a long row, with a corridor outside facilitating entry to each of the rooms.

In the rooms were various kinds of electronic equipment—Play Stations, televisions, mobile phones with no signals and a whole lot of advanced gaming consoles, as well as electric devices such as massage chair, virtual reality interface, beauty equipment and several objects of luxury.

Robots strolled around the rooms, patrolling the area. They weren't huge or driven by someone, but self-automated ones, with a white pot-like body and a black screen for a face, where eyes, eyebrows and mouth were digitally displayed in a shade of blue.

They moved with the help of small wheels. Ten of them lined up outside the glass rooms, blocking the entrance to the paradise of electronics.

Alex heard all ten of them speak together in a harsh voice—'Welcome to the sixth task: Technical Madness'.

\..\... `'

Chapter 12

Technical Madness

The robots parted, giving way for Lester and Alex to try some of the gaming devises.

Death risk had been one thing, technology was another. And now, luxury emerged as a new thing. But digital luxury was a mess. That's what both of them had stumbled into, and for which no plausible reason could be ascertained by either of them.

They had fun playing the terrific games and watching the adventurous movies. After winning nine out of ten matches of Tekken with Lester, Alex's eyes started hurting and his brain felt heavy. He tried to remember the purpose of their presence in that room. Surprisingly, he couldn't. Desperately, he tried to remember the formula of converting Celsius to Fahrenheit. He could not. He tried to remember his own name. He could not. Soon, the electromagnetic rays of *The-then-to-be-designed-in-future* virtual reality device burned through his retina, making his vision go blank.

'The same might've happened to Lester,' Alex renewed his storyline screenplay, imagining a black screenplay, as nothing was visible except darkness.

'The same might've happened to Lester,' Alex renewed his storyline screenpl... um... black screenplay... no. It has to be a storyline *audioplay* about the island's happenings... 'Yep. That's right.'

A sweet, hushed, soothing voice echoed in his mind.

'Welcome to...' The word 'ILLUSIONISTA' blazed through his mind, overlapping his newly acquired blindness.

'Yeah, so this isn't technical madness. It's an illusion. Wow. Maybe Lester is having another dream. Guess what, about fairies...? Nah.'

'But, hey, this raises possibilities. Maybe, just maybe, this whole thing of being on this island, the trip to Japan, everything is a disease I'm suffering from, in my sleep. All part of ILLUSIONISTA...'

With all of these thoughts going on in his head, he didn't realize that the illusion had brought alive a scene from his life.

'I surely hate this,' Alex braced himself.

The scene played up an old memory. He could see Uncle Edward's farm. It was a lovely evening. Cows strolled here and there, patrolling the farm, eating the grass.

Alex understood everything now—the confusion, or **Illusion**...

The technological room was part of the challenge, adopting features from the memories of Alex and Lester. The robots moving around were copied from the cows grazing in Uncle Edward's farm. They had been tricked by the robots, who gave them the fake title of the challenge. 'That might have been from Lester's memory,' Alex thought.

After Alex wrote his mindbook named *Sixth Mystery Uncovered*, the scene changed once again and he found himself in a movie theatre, with Lester sitting next to him.

The film running up on the Laserplex was disgusting. So, he spared the details from being added to his screenplay, and left it to the imagination of the readers instead. It may be violence fatality or...something else. One had to just think and it would have the *most-disgusting-thing-as-per-your-opinion* genre.

As they sat inside the theatre, their gazes were transfixed on the movie screen, and they watched the movie intently. After a few minutes, Alex noticed something unusual about the movie. Whenever dark colours came up on the screen, a transparent figure became visible.

'This is surely not a part of this film. It's something... something else...' he tried figuring it out. 'A rabbit? Nah. A... cheetah? Nope. A... turtle? Nope. A... something peculiar. And humongous. And powerful. Yeah. Got it. It's one of those weird animals.'

He now observed the animal carefully, ignoring the movie and the crackling noise of Lester munching his snacks. Alex didn't know how and when did they procure the snacks. The moment Alex started noticing the animal, it stared at him hard. Alex made a list in his mind, while being alert.

Dark green colour in background—ready to run.

Dark blue colour in background—two legs in the air.

Technical Madness

Maroon colour in background—not visible.

Now he understood that within a second or two, as the creature would pounce out of the screen, either Alex or Lester would be clawed at with the pressure of that penimal's (peculiar animal, which Alex recalled) jump.

He yelled, 'DUCK!'

Both of them rolled under their seats, only to see his seat ripped apart by sharp pointy claws. They ran furiously to get out of the theatre.

When they were out, they saw themselves in one of those rooms where those robots moved freely, with a wooden board labelled 'MOVIE THEATER' on the white wall behind them.

Alex stopped a robot and asked him where the exit was. In its usual harsh voice, it replied, 'Error' and fell face-first onto the ground.

'Wow. What's happening?' Lester said.

'No time to explain. Follow me.'

'Okay... but can't we just stop running for a while? Please slow down a bit.'

'No time. Let's get out of here.'

'I like games,' Lester mumbled.

At last they reached the end of the glass corridor. There stood a gigantic metal door coated with...

'Hibiscus flowers? No, rhododendrons? Nope, rust? Yeah. It's rust. So intimidating. Really, do the people who created this kidding?' Alex said.

On that door glinted a large golden... calculator...?

'Are they going to check our mathematical skills now? Are the robots gonna kill us if we fail to answer the questions correctly?' asked Lester, seemingly bothered.

On observing carefully, they saw that it wasn't a calculator, but resembled one. It had an '⏎' button, but no '=, +, -, × or ÷' signs. It also contained letters instead of numbers. On the screen blazed the word PASSSWORD. Lester looked like he'd been hit with a golf stick in the face.

'What could it be?' he asked incredulously.

'Umm... not sure.'

Lester cut him off.

'You mean you have it but are not sure?'

'I was saying "Not sure if I get this."'

Lester's face turned white. He looked quite nervous and restless now.

'So, bro, what do we do?'

'Work fast.'

'What are you talking about? Where... how... what work do we have to do fast...? What's this

ILLUSIONISTA that we saw earlier?' Lester enquired and added instantaneously, 'Hey, what if the password is ILLUSIONISTA itself?'

'Not possible. A password revealed so easily. Nah,' Alex replied thoughtfully.

After thinking for some time and thanking his stars for not running into any kind of danger in the meantime, he announced, 'Got it, I suppose.'

'Wha–? Got it? Hey, wait a minute. What do you mean by "I suppose"?'

'This is 13-word code, judging by the blank spaces in the calculator. I think it requires something that's relevant to the challenge,' replied Alex.

He filled it up with the words MOVIE-PENIMAL. He felt that this was the only plausible option.

'Should I press "enter"?' asked Alex.

'Not sure 'bout that.'

'Hey!'

Vigilantly looking at his backside, Alex saw a large volley of robots rushing towards them at about 30 miles per hour, portraying an angry face emoji on their digital faces.

'No option left. We have to do this right away,' Alex said to Lester.

Alex pressed ↵.

The surroundings went white. He saw himself in another of those sixty-four-dimensional places he'd encountered earlier, except that this one was totally white.

Chapter 13
Death Is Mandatory

Vishwaroopaha's booming voice echoed, encouraging Alex, 'Alex, now your tasks are getting harder and harder. Lester couldn't withstand them. He lost. Don't grieve for him. You can have him back. But the only condition is to get through to the ninth task. You'll meet Angelina at the starting of your ninth challenge. She will meet you after getting through her tasks. Together, you will have to face the ninth challenge to free Lester. The tenth one is to lift the curse off the people of this island. I hope you pass. Otherwise... death follows...' he ended, stressing the word *death*.

'Are you kidding?' Alex thought.

But it turned out to be true. Lester wasn't with him. His two companions from the very first challenge were fear and hopelessness, the latter given a boost by the loss of Lester and Angelina. 'Not forever...' he thought.

The place where Alex stood changed after Vishwaroopaha had spoken with his echoing voice. He found himself in an open dry grassland. It was dusk. Strong winds blew past him, sweeping dust from one place to another, making it difficult for him to keep his eyes open. A little later, Alex forced himself to open his eyes for a while. Lightning cracked the ground about a million times. Up above in the sky, Alex noticed some words displayed like a Power-Point presentation, except that the background template glowed due to the lightning windstorm. It went something like this:

| First five seconds |
WELCOME TO *The 7th DISASTER*

'Oh, great. Another name for one of these ten,' Alex noted.

| Next 5 seconds |
THIS IS A GAME WHICH YOU HAVE TO GET THROUGH WITHOUT GETTING KILLED. RULES ARE:

| Next 35 seconds |
YOU'LL GET THREE LIVES. IF ALL OF THEM ARE USED UP WITHOUT WINNING, YOU WILL EARN A ONE-WAY TRIP TO HELL!
THIS GAME IS NOT LIKE ANY OF THOSE MOBILE OR CONSOLE GAMES. JUST DO AS INSTRUCTED.
THERE ARE THREE LEVELS, ALL READY TO KILL YOU.
IF YOU LOSE A LIFE, YOU'LL HAVE TO START THE DISASTER FROM LEVEL 1.
GET READY FOR THE FIRST LEVEL. THERE IS GOING TO BE BLOOD.

Alex braced himself for bad luck. The PPT got over and the lightning windstorm continued. He tried to move, ready to figure out what just happened. But the game had begun. He couldn't move.

He looked down at his feet and noticed that they were locked to the ground by green and strong wooden tendrils arising from beneath the mud. Those root-like structures started getting a firmer hold of him, slowly climbing up his legs, waist and chest, and he could do nothing to stop them from encircling him.

The roots covered him fully, twisted around him, squeezing the blood out of him, resulting in the end of his first life. 'Gross,' he thought during his resurrection. 'I'd felt something like a hot ball of air combined with my stomach's digestive acids come up my throat. When that sensation got off, I lost my first life. Maybe I need to swallow it back and then fight the tentacles. Because sometimes,to achieve something, you need to be ready to face something *else*–something wholly different. I just can't figure out what those tentacles were, but that warm ball really caught my attention. Maybe it has been placed inside my 7th *Disaster*'s body to keep me distracted, away from the real threat of those green snake-like things.'

He started off with his second life. As he was plotting his next move, the tendrils came up to his chest and the ball started to form in his throat again. He swallowed it. It started vibrating awfully in his stomach, causing him to oscillate agonizingly. As a result the tendrils were shaken off him. As soon as they fell off, they disappeared in green smoke.

A minute later, it turned out that the ball of air was... actually... a fireball. It was extremely difficult to manage it inside his body; he felt a great pressure, as if his stomach would explode. Remembering his yoga skills, all of sudden Alex decided to go for a headstand and let it out through his mouth. The idea worked. He then sat up straight on the ground. For a minute, the fireball hovered in the air in front of Alex, as if trying to decide what to do with him. Then, as suddenly as it had sprung up, it hit him hard on the forehead, causing blisters on his skin.

Then there was silence and he lay there undisturbed. 'The level is complete, I suppose,' he assumed.

Waiting for the next level to come up, he curled up on the floor, exhausted and sleepy, trying to avoid the dust from getting into his eyes.

Alex was in for the next level.

But, unknowingly, he took a nap, and woke up to find himself on top of Mount Elbrus. He was shocked. Cold winds blew all around, threatening to freeze him to death.

He jumped. He didn't know why, but it happened quickly and spontaneously. He had no parachute. 'Sky fall with no parachute... Sounds better in a video game. But yeah, this is a real-life video game. But... what I really need is a parachute...' To his surprise, a parachute bag appeared on his back. He soon understood this level. He had to overcome his fear and use his imagination. He imagined the parachute opening up. It opened slowly, allowing him to land softly and hit the dirt. No. Not dirt. Snow. Almost immediately, the snow covered him fully, encasing him in an ice slab.

He willed it to melt, and it did. He willed himself to get to the third level and he did.

In the third level, he found himself swimming in the middle of an ocean. Nothing could be spotted as far as the eye could see. Not even a faint outline indicating the presence of a landmass.

Despite being able to swim, he drowned. 'Last life left. What do I do? Splash around uselessly? Needa think.'

He told himself that it was no use getting scared. He was desperate to find relevant clues to win over this level.

'Let it come', he faced everything with greater courage. He knew that this might be the last level for him, and didn't waver from the task at hand.

At that very instant, he thought that he was going to drown and die. Amazingly, he popped up to the ocean surface instead.

'It's reverse psychology,' he concluded joyously. 'Let's get through this level, too.'

No landmass was yet to be seen; he couldn't possibly use reverse psychology to be on Wasor again. 'But, I think I'm on Wasor right now, and not really in the ocean,' he assured himself, but soon doubted it. 'Or am I...?' At last, he decided, using reverse psychology, to lose hope, and deliberately thought that he would never get to the eighth disaster.

After a flash of an almost blinding light, he saw himself amidst a muddy battlefield. And it was night suddenly. Dead bodies were sprawled on the ground. The carcasses wore an armour, and blood dripped from their wounds.

'It seems that a battle has recently taken place.'

The people looked... Ancient... Indians? 'No guns were involved,' Alex found out, just by looking at the weapons and armour.

To his east and west was a forest. In the other two directions stretched the battlefield. 'A war...? Do I have to take someone's side and fight for him? Seriously, is this even a challenge?'

Alex waded through the cold air, walking straight ahead. He continued thinking, 'Well, if this is compulsory, then I have to get through this task, too. Would there be an option to take sides? If yes, then whom shall I support? What if I am not given any option at all?' sighing deeply he concluded, 'This all is too confusing and unpredictable.'

He soon found a saffron-coloured tent guarded by two soldiers at the entrance.

Alex ended up in a dialogue with himself.

Caring Alex, with reference to his recent thought, said, *You must get to that tent. Besides the hard work, you need hospitality.*

Working Alex countered, *Work is worship. I'll go with the right group that justifies the reason for war. Not just anyone who has better resources.*

Caring Alex agreed doubtfully, *But... will these tent guys welcome me if I try to get through them?*

Working Alex carelessly said, *Why not? After all, it's my challenge.*

Just as Alex returned to reality, he found himself walking towards the tent confidently, with a funny smile on his face. Maybe the **Working Alex** had hypnotized his whole being into making a fool of himself.

He stopped abruptly. The guards hadn't noticed him until then. He ducked behind a tree for a moment.

'I need to ask for shelter. How do I communicate with them?'

This question was a big hurdle, and set him back considerably.

He sighed and thought 'What's the harm in trying?'

'You'll embarrass yourself,' said a voice from behind. Alex turned back. There stood a man about Alex's age. His eyes were changing colours and patterns, like the colours of Wasor's animals and the ghost Vijaykarma. He wore blue jeans and a yellow T-shirt, with 'WASOR' written on it in green font. His facial expression was treacherously sweet.

'Hello. I'm a challenge guide for you. If you give me access to your body, I can translate your words to theirs and theirs to yours.'

'I know who a translator is. No need to say "Yours to theirs and theirs to yours". Anyway, why should I trust you?'

'I'm a registered trademark of Wasor Cursed Challenges. I'm at your service. Trust me, I'm not a trick. I'm totally genuine. Besides, you don't have any other option.'

Alex's situation forced him to accept the man's help. He said in a grudging tone, 'Permission granted.'

'Okay. Here you go.'

The man dissolved into a yellow fog, which then entered Alex through his nose. Letting him in, he thought, 'Couldn't he have another way to help me? Does he really have to get in through the nose? I wonder when he is gonna come out... Is he...? Or he's just going to stay there all his life... No, all my life?'

'At least this island provides some services. Hopefully, I shall be able to present myself smartly,' he thought at last.

He marched confidently up to the camp. 'This must be one of the sides. The other camp might be somewhere else,' Alex thought. 'Shall I enter? Is this the right side?' he thought looking all around him. 'No options for me to choose,' he replied to himself.

'Let me get in,' commanded Alex with confidence.

'Who are you?' one of the sentries asked, his spear raised.

'Easy... Is the king inside?'

'No.'

'Where can I meet him? I want to... um... give an important news to him,' he said. The guards eyed him suspiciously.

'He's at the palace.'

'Oh. Which way should I go, then?'

The guard pointed towards the forest. Alex pretended to move there to get out of sight. He knew the guards were bluffing. No king stays in the palace during war time, unless he has delegated someone to subdue a small army for him. Needless to say, by the looks of the battlefield, the war seemed to be almost over.

'I must pass the night in the woods. Tomorrow, after the day's battle, I'll ask the king to give me a position in his army,' he thought, as he lit a fire and sat on the cold ground in the forest. He was careful enough not to get lost, and avoided going too deep into it, staying in the vicinity of the camp.

'But... I'm not the fighting kind. Lester may have...' he sighed, as Lester's thought sprung up in his mind.

Annoyed, he thought, 'Okay. I'll have to plan cleverly. Talk to the king confidently and impress him. If I could somehow influence him intellectually or do something to become his favourite.... I must know the cause of the war at the earliest; it might help me understand this challenge better. That will be my motto tomorrow. Additionally, learning sword-fighting skills is the need of hour, or rather of this challenge. Though difficult, still I'm gonna do it.'

He tossed and turned all night thinking about this, only to be woken up at dawn by the king's troops, who had surrounded him, and had their spears pointed at him as he lay on the ground.

'What the hell are you doing?' he said.

'Hey, talk with respect. We are the king's *UchchSainikaha*,' Alex wondered why the translator hadn't converted this last word into English. 'Stupid fellow,' he thought.

At last, he said to the soldiers, 'Okay, okay. Sorry for sleeping here in the midst of wildlife. Is this your land? If not, then is this really your business?'

'Don't make us furious. Go away, strange clumsy man.'

Alex stood up and went to the other side of the forest, crossing the battlefield. 'Apparently today's war hasn't begun yet. Shocking,' he thought as he walked. He didn't know what to do. 'Arrogant. I hate these soldiers. I hope the king isn't like them. If he is, then I'd end up being imprisoned and hanged if I approach him. But... there's nothing I can do. Precisely, what can I do?'

'A helpful Vishwaroopaha, without his heartbreaking lectures, would have been perfect in this situation.' To reassure himself of his safety, he added, 'So plan changed. I'll show them the wonders of the latest science concepts, and blow their minds. Maybe *science* is the task... Lemme try my luck with gunpowder, if it is available around here. I'll talk to the king and science shall start it all... I'll help them win the battle through new techniques and head off to the ninth challenge. Besides, these people look good. Their culture looks good. Maybe this *is* the right side.'

So he went off to the camp to find inflammable substances, looking for something like gunpowder or alcohol.

'Need to blow off their enemies with a good technique.' He sneaked past the long and wide tent, keeping an eye on it while passing through the forest, and reached the tent's back entrance.

There was a grassland behind the tent. Some metal boxes were placed on it, and hundreds of swords and shields were piled up inside these boxes.

'This looks like their arms storage area. I need to find out what's in those boxes. It could contain the explosive items I am looking for,' Alex thought.

Unaware of the guards at the back entrance, he kept searching, as he was too engrossed planning his next move. He came out of the woods stealthily, his back arched and knees bent to hide behind the boxes in case the sentries came to check. But they were present there already, and Alex had failed to notice them.

But they saw him and yelled in unison, 'Hey!'

A moment later, Alex was presented before the king in the latter's tent, his hands bound by heavy metal chains. Alex didn't try to escape. He knew that if he got caught, he would get a chance to meet the king. The king wore ancient royal clothes, which Alex had seen in many of *Mahabharata*'s digital clips when he visited India. Truly, travelling made him knowledgeable.

The king sat on a highly embellished magnificent throne. Every detail of it mesmerized Alex. His gaze was interrupted by the words of magnanimous king, who was surrounded by his men.

'Who are you? What's your purpose?'

Alex understood the impracticality of telling the truth to him. So, he made up a story, which he realized later, was far weirder than the things that had happened to him until then.

'I'm a traveller from the future,' he said, looking straight into the eyes of the king, leaving no reason to be disbelieved.

Death Is Mandatory

'I... um... kind of fell into a black chasm-like pit from a mountain and found myself in your time, in that jungle. I tried to ask for shelter yesterday, but your guards made me back off. By the way, what year is it?'

'Your story does not sound credible. How do I believe you?' his eyebrows lifted up as he looked at Alex. 'But by the looks of your clothes and your appearance, I guess, in some way or the other, you might be speaking the truth. The year right now is 1265 CE,' he added after Alex gave him an innocent expression.

'If it's 1265 CE right now as per the Indian calendar, it means that Vishwaroopaha is somewhere in this era, too. If these people know him, then I would be happy to inform these hostile... no, not hostile people... They don't seem to be hostile, but they are not quite friendly either. They're just... whatever. I would like to convey to them that I am his friend. That will give me an opportunity to get enrolled in service,' he thought and acted up on his plan.

'O benevolent king, I pledge all my life, might and loyalty to you and your kingdom. I shall be highly privileged if you assign me a post in your administration as I'm not well-versed in the art of sword fighting,' he faked a pledge while keeping his fingers crossed, trying to slump his shoulders down to portray sadness.

'How can I trust you?'

'O lord, until you find me of use, I promise that I will not harm you or any of your minions in any way,' he said at last.

'Okay. Good for you. You better not even dare to harm us. You seem... untrustworthy. You'll be in the custody of my soldiers until you prove yourself worthy of something. You'll have to meet me tomorrow in the morning. Until then, you must think of something to save yourself from punishment, because you trespassed into our tent. Follow all the orders given to you, and abide by them. By the way, what's your name and where do you belong to?'

'I am Alex Drake, born in Florida in the year 1989 CE.'

'Dismissed.'

Being dragged away by a powerful bunch of muscular guards while bound in chains wasn't really Alex's idea of having fun. He was being taken to another tent, away from the king's throne.

The soldiers glared at him and then at each other, as if having a discussion about him, something like...

Wanna slice that guy's head? He smells nasty.
I dunno. Ask the emperor.

As he stood there, Alex racked his brain for an amazing act to pop up in his mind. But, for that he needed to break free. Alas, he had no such luck. 'Hey, bad luck, can't you just leave me, like, *for this whole challenge?*' he pleaded in his mind.

Surprisingly, he remembered something. Something amazing enough to stun the guts out of the king.

'Voice Conductor'

Alex focused on the Voice Conductor's concept. He could almost imagine him speaking, 'When we talk, our vocal cords make molecules in the air vibrate. Inside our ears are tiny sensitive hair. They pick up the vibrations and transmit that information to our brains, which interpret it as sound. Using this technique, we can communicate easily even if we are very far away. For this we need two cups and a string. We have to punch a small hole at the bottom of each cup, right in the centre, and thread one end of the string through the bottom of the cups, and fix the thread in place. Two people have to hold the cups. One has to speak through it while the other has to press his ear to it. In this activity, the person's voice will vibrate the air inside of the cup, which will make the bottom of the cup vibrate. These vibrations will be transferred to the string and then onto the other person's cup, which will make the air inside of his or her cup vibrate and become a detectable sound.'

'That little trick with two cups and a rope. Yeah, that's the spirit, buddy!' But as he was about to call for the king's attention that he'd just achieved his way out of those chains, he wondered why he hadn't asked the king's name. 'He kept himself anonymous... Why? Kings usually feel a sense of pride when they affix their names after the word "The Great"... Something's fishy. Maybe it's just the translator. Never mind.'

Waving off these thoughts, he warned himself, 'Future will be changed if that technique is disclosed. Indians will be really powerful in their region. They will conduct various expeditions and reach the US before Vasco da Gama. They will wage wars. If they succeed, they'll rule the world by spying through this technique. If these people are exposed to the nuances of science in this early era, maybe I wouldn't even exist. Neither would my family.'

He understood the task. It was not to take someone's side to fight for; it was to think of something creative while being careful about not making the slightest change in future. 'Vishwaroopaha was right. The tasks are getting harder and harder. My friends aren't capable of facing them. I recall how they cowered in a corner in the second challenge,' misery flowed over him.

'Where are they now? What must they be going through at this moment? I really don't have the courage to even think,' he burst out into a sob as he thought of them. It drew the guards' attention.

'Too scared, spy? You managed to fake your way out of our king's grasp, eh? But you'll not be able to escape us without proof,' one of them exclaimed.

'For your kind information, I'm not a spy. I am not even from this century or a few succeeding this! I have stumbled into this island from future! Now, please, let me think of ways to prove myself. And I beg you, don't tease me anymore.'

'As you wish, *spy.*' Both of them had a hearty laugh.

'Done? Now can you mind your own business?' Alex replied sarcastically.

Fortunately, this silenced them. 'Seems like, these two haven't witnessed sarcasm yet. Poor people,' Alex thought pitifully. But the episode meant that the little window of time he had to show his skills to the king had gone to waste.

'Am I really supposed to be killing time?' he asked himself. A part of his mind answered, *Nah. Kill yourself out of this mess.*

What?

Nothing. Think of something to get through this challenge.

As he was having this internal argument, he heard the sounds of swords clashing with armour and shields, mixed with the noises of war cry. The battle had begun. This was the perfect moment for Alex. But to do what? To kill himself? He didn't know.

'Something drastic has to be done by me right now,' he had a gut feeling.

But what? His mind, which had always been packed with gut-busting ideas, went blank. 'What happens to me at crucial times?' he asked himself.

'Should I strangle these guards and launch myself into the battle? Nope. That would be stupid.' He closed his eyes and thought. He sprang up from his imaginary workshop suddenly, as he felt a cold metal hitting him hard in the legs and then on the head. He blacked out and fell onto the ground, stricken with shock and intolerable pain.

'I dunno why I am memorizing all the gross and unfair things that have happened to me till date. If Lester were with me, he would've been like *Hey, bro, isn't there another activity going on there? Like a basketball match or a video game contest?* If there was any girl from my teenage friend group, she'd say, *It's too gross! Can't there be a butterfly-chasing excursion in that jungle, or at least a little less treachery and rudeness?* Yeah, I know this all. But, this place is a lot friendlier than I thought. And, to be honest, I even don't know why it's named Wasor. *Wasor* and *Weird* both begin with a 'W', probably that's why? One must go figure it out. Maybe Vishwaroopaha would tell us... us? Lester... he sighed.

'Anyway, beware. Bring up a bunch of candies to stop you from blacking out. I think the world is going to get crueller!' he cautioned, imagining that *someone* would be watching him, having a good laugh about his sufferings.

Alex woke up later, sprawled on the floor. 'Do I really have to be knocked unconscious all the time?' he thought, pitying himself.

No one seemed to be in the tent when he looked around, still lying down.

Suddenly, a heat wave caught Alex's attention. He saw that the saffron cloth shelter, in which he lay, was burning from all sides, with each part engulfed in flames. He stood up to run.

But, he realized that there was no way to get out.

'Wow. I'm gonna be dead soon. I'll never be meeting my friends or parents! It's the end! The end of my life! Yay! But... now I'm not gonna waste time to cry, or sob or whatever,' he tried to put up a brave front.

He then went berserk trying to enjoy the last moments of his life, skipping around in the tent, recalling old and happy memories. As he was completing his eighth circle, fatefully, a trapdoor opened beneath his feet, causing him to slide down through a rectangular steel tube. He slid and slid further down, thanking his luck.

'Hey, but the things would get crueller,' the one watching him may say, Alex remembered. *'I have brought up my favourite candies. But it's not that cruel. Alex isn't suffering bad luck!'*

'Yeah, I know.' replied Alex, waiting till he got to the end of the trapdoor. 'And... and... it's true. I'm really not suffering bad luck. I must put away my candies now.'

'Phew, I saved myself from going bonkers.

Saved... Yes, I am safe! This place reminds me of childhood. Those swings, the slide... yes... good days. I love my luck! It isn't so bad after all,' Alex thought, regaining some courage and strength.

But poor Alex didn't know what awaited him at the other end of the passageway. He ended up being dumped in a dark dumpster. There was something extraordinary about the place. Alex looked down and saw bones, dead bodies and skeletons strewn everywhere, just as he was. Dumped. And it was an extremely undignified experience.

The incident came as a bolt from the blue. His hope to survive was shattered, and he could visualize his skeleton lying in the heap—unwanted and anonymous.

Chapter 14

The Dumpster of the Dead

With utmost difficulty, he regained his vigour and thought process. 'The ruler of that kingdom might have killed his prisoners and dumped them here. But, how do I get out of this place? Yes, I failed to prove myself in the challenge. This might've been my punishment. A living creature dumped–,' thought Alex.

He was cut off by a heavy male voice, deep enough to vibrate the spinal cord out of anyone, '–in the Dumpster of the Dead. Yeah, this is my pavilion. No living organism can leave this place unscathed.'

Then he revealed himself, casually walking amidst the skeletons and occasionally kicking the bony carcasses.

The Dumpster of the Dead

He too was a skeleton, like the ones piled up next to Alex's feet, but about five times their size. Alex looked up. It seemed that the height of the room was specifically designed for this skeleton. A dark green light shone around him, making him visible. He looked scary, too scary. Alex thought for a moment that he might've seen flashes of blood-red light on his face. At the same time, the skeleton's head seemed to be splattered by blood.

'Perhaps, green is the sacred colour of Wasor. The Beauties also used a cauldron filled with green liquid,' Alex tried to think, and the words poured out of his mouth spontaneously.

'Yes. That's true. I was made by your friends' acquaintance traits with you, through which I gained knowledge about you, your life, the way you behave when you are with your friends, the trust you have in them and your willingness to do anything for them. That was combined with that magical green liquid. The kingdom, tent, translator and the rest was crafted by me. This challenge is nothing but me. You can't think anything here, clever Alex. It has to come out of your voice box. I know everything about you. My name is Bonzrehmenna.'

'So... you wanna fight? Or... kill me with your powers?' asked Alex, terrified at the sight of the creature, trying hard to speak bravely.

'See, I want nothing from you. I just need your soul,' he spoke in a heavy, commanding voice. 'If you are capable of walking after that, you are free to leave,' he said, gesturing towards a dark spot, free of bodies.

He continued further, looking at Alex's confused expression, 'Oh, you don't see anything? I feel sorry for your ignorance. Defeat me and escape. There's a door right there in that spot. Only the dead can see it. '

'What do you want?' Alex replied, whimpering badly. He wet his pants. A wise choice, indeed.

Bonzrehmenna (Alex decided to call him Bonz for short) zoomed rapidly towards Alex and struck him in the weak spot with his bony hand, but soon withdrew.

'Pee-yoo! I hate it! Yuck! But yes, it shows you fear me,' he said, smiling crookedly.

Alex dodged and looked around for something that could help him fight Bonz. No luck. He was stunned by a bone with which Bonz hit him on the head, leading him to spin in all directions. Instinctively, he grabbed a stone embossed on the wall.

The Dumpster of the Dead

'Get away from that!' Bonz shouted as he kicked Alex in the stomach. Alex moved away, unaware of his hand's grip on the stone. He twisted it like a doorknob as he fell.

'Wow. I just opened the door to get out,' he thought, but in vain. He realized it wasn't a doorknob but a stone, and perhaps he accidentally removed it.

Bonz replied, 'No! You, nincompoop! By removing that stone, you have destroyed my dumpster. Now both of us will die. This roof will crash!'

'Nope. I have an advantage. You are five times my size. You'll hold up the top of this room while I will use the door to get away.'

'No... no, you can't...' Bonz was stopped by the heavy weight of the rooftop piling on his shoulders. He tried to hold it up with both his hands.

Alex moved around, looking for the door. He remembered that it would open only if Bonz was defeated. He decided to sit in a corner to be safe from the falling rubble, waiting for Bonz to sink beneath the boulders. Soon, Bonz collapsed beneath the stones. The roof opened up but no sunlight came through. It was completely dark.

'Is it night? A new moon day? It's just...' while thinking about the time of day, Alex somehow managed to walk over the dusty rock surface littered with bones.

Suddenly a part of the room shook heavily. A portion of the wall crumbled off, leaving behind a golden elevator. Alex went straight in, instinctively knowing that this was the way to head towards the ninth challenge. There were no floor-selecting buttons, neither the ">|<" nor the "<|>" buttons for opening and shutting the doors. The only button was "□". Alex pressed it without a second thought.

He zoomed upward rapidly as the elevator's doors slid shut. On the floor-display screen, two words blazed: NINTH DISASTER.

Soon, the elevator reached the destination for his ninth challenge.

The moment Alex got out of the elevator, it dissolved into thin air behind him. He found himself in his school's playground, and was amazed at how frequently the locations changed while he was making his way through the challenges.

'It's been so long since I've been here!' he thought. He noticed Angelina a few metres away, rummaging through her handbag. He was overjoyed to see her again.

He moved to a spot behind her and tapped her shoulder for attention. 'Hello!'

She shrieked so loudly that her voice echoed off the school walls. 'Relax, it's me,' Alex comforted her as she turned towards him.

'Oh... Alex.' She hugged him. Angelina seemed fazed by something. She had scars on her face and hands, few of them still fresh and bloody. Her touch made Alex realize that she'd gone through a lot; her skin was very cold to touch. She looked startled and disturbed. 'Where had you been? I have been looking for you all around! You prankster!'

'I hadn't been away. You were separated by a large ball-like rock from the two of us.'

'Two...,' she glanced around, her eyes looking for Lester.

'Yeah... Lester's not here. This challenge is for both of us to find him.'

'Okay. You know what, I...'

'I know we have a lot of individual experiences to share. But first, let's kick the butts out of these remaining two tasks.'

'You're right. Let's move on.'

'Chop chop.'

'Yeah, chop chop,' Angelina smiled.

The phrase was normal, but it added a bit of humour to the drab scenario. It was a hard situation, yet Alex hadn't lost his knack of joking, which he had learnt from Lester.

| Florida |

'What are you doing?' Clinton asked as he looked at Eric, who sat silent as if meditating deeply.

'Nothing. Get ready. I have a feeling something is going to happen. I sense that... Lester's in trouble. Let's hurry. They have asked us to get into the aircraft. Move, move!' Eric replied, still tensed.

All three of them trudged towards AF 13 098. It was a ten-seater, multi-engine, twin-prop airplane. Before getting in, the aircraft assistant told them about the plane's parachute facilities and evacuation plan.

'We needa hurry,' Clinton exclaimed.

The pilot cranked up the engine. Soon, they were miles away from Florida. Eric said, 'We've come up all this way in a hurry, and haven't thought of some critical factors.'

'Like what?' Clinton asked.

'Even though we have to take an aerial survey before landing, I don't think there would be an airstrip on that island. We'll have to jump with the help of parachutes. This very thought is worrying me. What'll happen next? No one knows. I hope we land safely and initiate our plan of rescue.'

'Don't worry, sir! We have the most advanced parachutes and you shall be guided well to have a safe landing. I can assure that,' interrupted the pilot.

| BACK TO SCHOOL! |

Alex was happy to be back in St. Paul's School. He wished to show Angelina his class and where he sat during classes. Usually he was a backbencher, in order to avoid interruptions to the *brainy* pranks played by him. He spoke of how he played pranks, and went on and on talking about his school days. He wanted her to accompany him to the auditorium, games room and research labs.

As soon as Alex finished showing Angelina the first floor of his school, she interrupted hesitatingly,

'Uh... you know, we are in for some tasks. We must really get all our attention into retrieving Lester.'

'You're right, but–'

'Say nothing.'

'The–'

'No.'

'Okay. Let's move to the second floor.'

Angelina raised her eyebrow. 'I think I hear someone weeping.'

'Which direction?'

'There.' She pointed towards the Physics Lab.

Alex spat. 'I'll never go there again, even if I am given double my dad's wealth. I was busted for carrying chits during practical exams.'

'Do you need Lester or you can carry on without him?'

'Of course I want that joker back!'

'Then follow me.'

Alex grumbled about how bad he was feeling without Lester, and followed Angelina. They went inside. Angelina said, 'I can't hear it now.' She scouted the room, scanning each object.

Alex said, 'We need to find a secret entrance leading to Lester's prison. There's always a secret entrance.'

'I hope you're right.'

Both of them investigated for some clue.

Soon Alex was exhausted. He sat on the floor, feeling helpless. Sure, Angelina was back, but Lester was lost. It was agonizing. Earlier Lester was with Alex, but Angelina was lost.

He closed his eyes in desperation. All of sudden he fell asleep and saw Lester in his dream, sad and pleading for help. He woke up with a start. 'How long have I been...?' he asked Angelina, who was looking around frantically.

'Two minutes.'

'Wha–?'

'Now, get up and look around.'

Alex noted that Angelina had developed a strong determination. She had transformed into a better and mature person. Her behaviour had changed and she seemed quite concerned about Lester, concentrating hard to find him. He decided to follow her plan.

When Alex looked around, he saw a closet. He opened it up. Besides various items, such as exam papers and physics apparatus, he saw a noticeable object that was different from the others. It was labelled as **9**. He found it to be a puzzle game box.

It comprised several locks bound together by a rope, with keys attached together in a ring. The instruction manual said:

[Welcome to the ninth task. You must pick the correct keys for the locks. If you fit any of them wrongly, then the number of wrong guesses will end up as the number of metal chains on your friend's neck, whom you both are searching. A digital screen will tell you if you're right or wrong. Guess the correct key to each lock, and you'll get a path to find your comrade.]

Alex called Angelina and hurriedly showed the instructions to her.

'Oh, God. We need to do something. Fast. T-That chain thing...' she stammered tensely.

'It's what we gotta do,' Alex replied courageously.

He observed something.

'Let's see...' He tried to open one of the locks with a key, as the shape of the keyhole and the key tip looked similar. It didn't open. The screen displayed—'***Wrong***'. Suddenly, they heard Lester's loud screams from... nowhere.

'Oh no,' Alex apologised to Angelina.

The Dumpster of the Dead

Angelina had an angry expression on her face, and soon, she burst into tears.

Alex didn't bother to sympathize. He needed much of it himself. He decided to focus on the puzzle rather than her sobs. Observing carefully, he noticed that the locks were 26 in number. The keys, naturally, were the same in number, too. 'Hmm... twenty-six words on the locks... and numbers from one to twenty-six on the keys... It has some relation to the English alphabet, I think... hmm... Isn't it, Angelina?'

'I bet you're right. But there're words on locks, not letters... like this lock says 'COW', Angelina said, pointing to a lock. 'Each of the words has an odd number of letters—COW, OCEAN, SUNNY. I wonder why. And the keys, they bear numbers... Hey, look at this... this lock has just one letter... "I". Mind if I try number 9? "I" is the ninth alphabet in the English language.'

'Okay. But watch out. We can't risk Lester's life anymore,' replied Alex.

'I don't know why I'm doing this. But I feel it's the right thing to do,' saying this Angelina tried to fit in lock I with key 9.

The lock opened and the screen displayed—**'*Correct*'**.

That got Alex's brain working. He figured out that the middle letter of each word on the lock was paired with the key that bore the corresponding number of the English alphabet. He then fitted each key to the locks.

The ground disappeared in a flash, and they found themselves in a muddy cavern, with stairs leading upwards. There was no fresh air. No sunlight. It was pitch dark.

'No. Not again!' Alex said, annoyed.

'What?' Angelina asked, apparently confused.

'Nothing. Let's go. Though I don't like caves and darkness, still, I'll go first,' he said and went up the stairs. As he placed his foot on the first step, two cracks appeared on it, one on each side of his foot, and lava came pouring out, covering half of the step.

He said to Angelina, 'Hurry! Come up fast!' As he said so, he tried to put as little weight as possible on the steps to slow down the intensity of the cracks, and ran up hurriedly. Angelina came quickly after him. When Alex looked back down at the stairs, they were smouldering under the lava. He helped Angelina get down from the topmost step by offering his hand. 'These steps were made to sink our feet in lava. We've defeated them,' said Alex.

The Dumpster of the Dead

'No, Not really. My left foot is hurting...' Angelina replied.

'Oh. Will you be able to walk?

'No. I am hurt. But I can try limping with your support.'

'Here,' he helped Angelina limp her way till... It was the same cavern where sunlight peeped through the gaps between the elegant stone walls. As Alex and Angelina scooted off to the cavern, they saw something.

Both of them knew Lester would be in a cage, with a heavy metal chain bound around his neck. He might be struggling to free himself. They had anticipated that the cage might be guarded by someone. Crocodiles? Gorillas? Giant spiders? They didn't know.

'Nah. This isn't it,' thought Alex.

Lester was sprawled on the floor with a heavy metal chain around his neck, his face lying flat on the ground. His 'room' was similar to a prison cell. What startled them was that Lester wasn't in a single cell. He was present in ten of them, which were lined horizontally.

Alex shouted, 'It's all duplicated. We'll need to find the right one.'

'But what if we fail?'

'No consequences have been defined,' he added reluctantly. 'In that case, I am afraid the chains will magically work their way through Lester's neck.'

'Oh, boy.'

'This is the ninth challenge. The correct cell will be the ninth one. Yes!'

'Okay, but... from left or right?' Angelina expressed her doubt.

'This is the mission to free Lester. Hmm...' he thought for a moment and then continued, 'He always said "right is always right". It must be... it's ninth from the right and second from the left. Yep. That's it.'

Angelina asked him how could they free him.

He thought for a while and said, 'That's where we're stuck. Don't know how to get in.'

'How will we get back after freeing Lester out of the prison?' questioned Angelina.

'Okay. That's another area where we're stuck.'

'Do you care wondering why there are ten of these?' Alex asked.

'To confuse us, dumbo.'

'Yeah. That's right. But, if it's just only that, then fine. M-my... my final doubt—If we've to get in, then...'

he paused. 'I'm not able to form the words. I just need to investigate.'

'Okay. Go on.'

Alex went up to the rightmost prison cell. As he peered through the metal-rod wall, it disappeared. Subsequently, the image of Lester also faded. Alex stepped in. The cell turned out to be an illusion, which disappeared.

'Hey, join me here!' he called Angelina, who was picking her nose.

She followed him as he explored the other cells. When he looked at a wall through the bars or at a Lester, both would disappear. At last, he found himself in the eighth cell from the right. As usual, a wall and a Lester dissipated in air. He then looked through the room of the ninth cell.

He saw that some of the bars dissolved, but some remained there.

'We need to squeeze through. If someone wouldn't be cautious enough, he could casually bang his head against these metal rods,' he said to Angelina. They did as planned. Alex was finally able to see his friend.

He kneeled before Lester and shook him vigorously. But, even after multiple attempts, Lester didn't wake up.

'Let's take this chain off him,' Alex said.

As soon as he touched it, he was forced to withdraw his hand. A drop of Alex's sweat had fallen on the chain, which immediately turned into vapour. The chain was quite hot to touch.

'The temperature is *too* high. Perhaps this is the last hurdle of this challenge; whoever comes to rescue Lester shall feel such high temperatures,' said Angelina. 'I have the perfect device for this.'

She pulled out a toy gun from her hand bag.

'A toy gun?' Alex was bewildered.

But the gun spewed ice flakes instead, as Angelina used it to bring down the chain's temperature, subsequently pulling it off him.

'Cool. Where did you get it?' Alex remarked.

'Long story.'

'Yeah... I understand. Mine is also a long story.'

'But you don't possess anything! I mean... you have no... no prizes! No souvenirs!'

'What's the need for souvenirs? You wanna remember these experiences? If I had a large handbag like you, I would've brought a large 100-pound skeleton head!' he retorted.

'Oh my gosh...'

'Anyway, let's go.'

The Dumpster of the Dead

'Where? You said that there's another field where we're stuck.'

'Um... we'll deal with that later. First, let's get out of this "Ten-cage puzzle",' saying this, Alex picked up Lester and left the prison.

'Lester is really heavy. Believe me, I'm bearing this man's weight for the second time in a day,' he remarked as he plopped him on the ground.

'Now what? Move on further? We can't possibly get back wading through the lava, even with my *coldy-guy*. I've named it so. What? Don't look at me like that. I know you'll start teasing me for naming it so. Anyway, the stairs had disappeared then and there. We can't go back. That's what I'm trying to say,' Angelina told Alex in an anxious tone, just as he had started laughing in the middle of her talk.

'Look... I know we're stuck but... I can feel some bad vibes. Some unusual power lies on the way back. We both know that the magic element isn't a fool. I mean, it won't let us get through. After all, we've just completed the ninth task, and don't know how we'll get to the next level. The magic, huh, as called by us, I think, is planning something big...' Alex replied thoughtfully.

'Yeah, you're right. Both of us know that the magic, or whatever it is, isn't a doofus. But look here, we have another doofus who doesn't know that,' saying this in an informal joyous tone, Angelina bent down and stroked Lester's hair. 'Cute. Isn't he?'

'No time for all this.'

'You and your time! It's driving me nuts! We haven't been at peace for a while now. Can't we rejoice a little for reuniting with our dear friend?' annoyed, Angelina spoke at one go. Then taking a deep breath she said, 'Fine. Move on. If you see or suspect anything, let me know.'

As Alex moved one step forward to investigate the area, he saw a trail of red colour on the ground. He held up Lester by the shoulders and signalled Angelina to follow him while he followed the splattered colour. He continued walking for a long time although his legs had started to wobble.

Out of exhaustion he fell down, Lester's weight burdening upon him now. He noticed that the floor he fell on wasn't the same muddy one on which he had been walking on earlier, and some part of it had changed into a thin surface, similar to paper. It was not just regular paper; it was rough and strong

The Dumpster of the Dead

enough to hold up their weight, only to reveal later that its surface was covering the mouth of a large ditch below.

Alex fell down, face-first on the paper. He saw some words on it..., written with... red paint? Nope.

The colour looked darker than red. It seemed to a very dark shade of red paint; the only other plausible conclusion could be that the words were written in blood. Yes. Blood.

The trail of red colour that Alex followed emerged from the letter 'Y', from the word 'YOUR'.

Alex made sure that he was able to decipher the meaning behind the text, and was not merely reading it.

Soon, he noticed two words.

YOUR DEATH

That's when something incredible happened.

Incredible, in the sense of defeat and negativity, and not success and positivity.

Angelina scooted up and stood adjacent to Lester and Alex's fallout place. She looked down at Alex and asked, 'Are you okay?'

'Yeah, it seems I am, but this place isn't. And Lester, too...' replied Alex.

As he glanced at the word DEATH, he was stunned and scared, anticipating something unforeseen.

'Hey, Angelina... my hand, you see, as I fell, landed on the bloodied word YOUR while you're standing on...' he said as his voice faltered and he became wide-eyed.

Angelina turned cold. She completed Alex's speech...

'**DEATH**,' she said this in a tone that was definitely not hers. It was a male, metallic, booming, raspy and touching voice, as if it were some mechanical structure's clinks combined with the hissing of snakes and two deadly, raspy voices in an old audio recording.

Death isn't referred to as a dead corpse here, neither a video player showing murders and not Thanatos or Hades. In panic, Alex, tried to wake Lester up, tossing and turning him here and there.

Suddenly, Angelina transformed into a demon, a she-demon with large black wings and red eyes. But she looked far scarier than those seen on comic-book covers or horror movies.

Angelina started to get used to her new demon form, muttering, 'Hey! Wha–' This time it was her normal voice. But it changed to that terrifying one, as if she were possessed and was trying to get back to her body, 'Okay. I've got to kill Alex and his companion. Let's do this. You're not going to leave the island alive, Alex! This will not end in a close call!'

'Angelina, you're gonna kill me? Hey! It's me! Alex!'

Alex then pulled out the spikes, which were stuck to the leather piece, from his pocket. He had pocketed them when the fifth challenge ended.

'It had been quite rough and irritating keeping these. Thank God! At last I can use them! While she's busy exploring her new character Angelina Demon aka AD, lemme torture Lester again!' He thought and smacked the spikes in Lester's stomach.

'It might hurt him but it's worth it. He needs to wake up. He made us suffer... No, not us... just me. Because... Angelina's a demon! She's going to kill me! Yeah, I really mean it. I'm dead. She's striki–,' his random thoughts were interrupted as Lester woke up.

Just then, the paper holding their weight came crashing down, and the three of them fell deeper and deeper... 'Maybe she was just trying to test—*Is this a hazardous dream?*—by whacking me. But she seems totally different... dunno what is happening to her...?' Alex tried to think.

It turned out to be a never-ending fall, plummeting them down at great speed. Alex was tired. AD continued to claw at Lester and Alex, ripping the paper with her mighty fingernails, while Alex and Lester tried to drift as far away as possible.

'Hey, bro! Whaddya doin'? This is a tough situation, but that won't stop me from being casual. By the way, thanks for freeing me.' Lester asked a series of questions, as he pushed out a bit of paper from his mouth.

'Doing nothing, just getting bored.' replied Alex ironically.

'D'ya know when we'll reach the tenth challenge?'

'Nah.'

All of sudden, Alex started feeling nauseous, and his vision changed. Now, he could only spot multiple hexagonal images. He saw the world as:

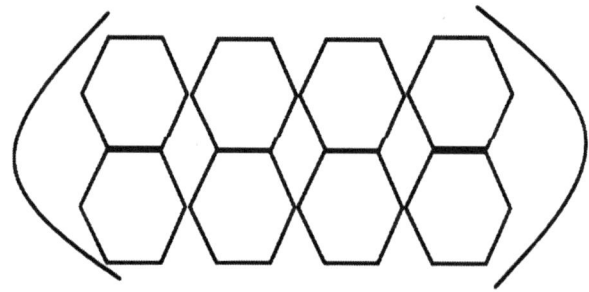

It appeared like a honeycomb-framed pair of glasses. Though Lester was snappy with the same effect, Alex wasn't even fazed. He thought of this as completely normal, given that it was the tenth challenge.

At last, all of them stopped falling, just in time to drown in... honey. AD, being heavier, sunk deeper. Alex managed to bring Lester to the surface of the honey pool. The surroundings were discomforting.

The sun blazed high up in the clear sky. Alex, with his best pal Lester, was in a pond of honey, around which were beehives, with thousands of bees milling around in the air. The pond was surrounded by a glass wall. The outer side of the wall appeared to be guarded by another huge swarm of bees. The glass reservoir of honey was in the middle of a crocodile-infested water pond. Beyond the pond was a large desert, and to their astonishment, there lay about a thousand poison ivy, with their branches sticking out of the hot sand.

Alex felt forlorn and lost, the worst he had felt so far. He glanced at Lester, who was taking huge gulps of air, as had developed a new kind of sensitivity from the surroundings.

The situation they were in was far worse than Alex could have imagined. It seemed to be equal to five more challenges, lying in wait for him and Lester. Plus, AD was on their tail. She could get them anytime soon.

This all was well laid. It really is...' he didn't have words to explain his condition. 'I guess this honeycomb effect will wear off when I get out of here,' he muttered to himself.

Surprisingly, Lester heard this. He said, 'Did you just say honeycomb effect? Yup, that's got me, too. Relax, bro. You're not the only one suffering.'

Lester was a positive guy, which was something Alex liked about him. But time acted savage on this island. Alex couldn't relax. He was in a state of continuous shock and panic. And he was extremely nervous.

He was low on energy, so he consumed honey—a lot of it. Lester copied him, and it cured him off the sensitivity.

The honey, when gulped by Alex, was enough to make him unconscious. The sweet, sticky, stale and smelly honey was too heavy to handle. Alex started feeling its effect on him. But Lester's case was different.

'Lester already suffered from a sensitivity and the honey cured him. Now it's all up to him. I am wholly dependent on his disposal for the hardest of the challenges. When I'm... if I'm alright again, I would find myself at the end of the tenth challenge, or... or in hell. Fate, I'm all yours!' noted Alex, before blacking out, the sticky honey piling over him like quicksand.

\..\... `'

Chapter 15

Let's Wriggle Out!

After a thousand moments of being semi-consciousness, Alex finally became aware of his senses. A lot of honey had splattered over him. He saw Lester screaming in pain, clutching his nose. He noticed AD swinging her arms, legs and wings madly, splashing honey in all directions like missiles. Sometimes she rolled up hundreds of bees in her hands, and threw them like shot-put balls, cursing them. It was a total chaos.

Alex finally realized that Lester was up to nothing, and was just wasting time. They were still trapped in the glass enclosure.

Night had come up to take sky's duty, and the bees were silent.

Let's Wriggle Out!

Alex had been thinking of ways to get out of the pond. In a while he came up with an idea. He figured out that he could take advantage of AD's madness to attack the honeybee household, and escape from the glass-walled room. But he needed a safety plan to prevent everyone from becoming a feast of the hungry crocodiles. It would be the hurdle waiting for them, as soon as they would break through the glass room. Hopelessness took over him yet again.

He patted himself everywhere, searching for a helpful clue. It was really hard to move even an inch in that sticky mess, but Alex managed to do it somehow. When he reached for his shirt pocket, he felt the three badges. He groped around his shirt until he felt the new one, unpinned it and brought it out of the pool of honey. He then examined it carefully.

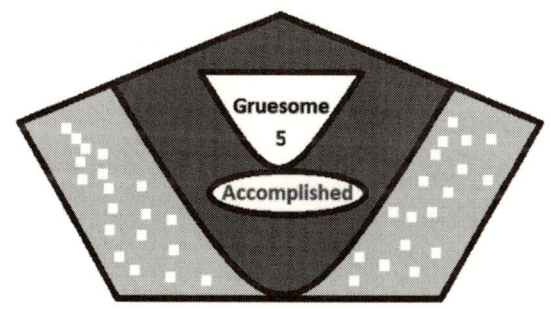

As soon as he placed the badge on his palm, it spewed mud slowly and made a muddy ground on the surface of his hand, holding a few shrubs on it. 'This ought to make a separate safe ground for me and Lester while AD handles those fierce crocs,' he planned.

Something drew Alex's attention. 'How come the badge was the prize meant for only five challenges? Why not nine?' he wondered. But, this added to his perception that as the tasks were getting harder, it was becoming harder to win a badge. Alex hoped to finish the last challenge soon and receive the last badge, too.

'As for now, it's time to make the bees aggressive!' Alex said softly as he quietened Lester down, who was continuously complaining about the bee stings on his nose.

Alex instructed, 'Hold your breath and dip yourself in honey'.

'*What?*'

'Just do it.'

'For how long do I need to do so?' he asked.

'Um... no clue.'

'You're crazy,' said Lester, as he buried himself in honey.

Let's Wriggle Out!

Alex cracked his knuckles. 'Let's do this.'

He then fired blobs of honey at AD's face, who was at the other end of the room. This made AD angrier, but she didn't notice that it was done by Alex. Luckily, she didn't mutter abuses, as her mouth was stuffed with honey. Besides annoying AD, this action of Alex made the bees more aggressive. Both AD and the bees fought in their *stinging ways* with each other.

It was the last scene that Alex saw before he went under honey. Thereafter, the glass walls broke due to AD's thrashing wings, emptying all of the honey into the pond, and drowning glass pieces, bees and AD in it.

Without making further delay, Alex quickly yanked Lester up and threw the third badge on the largest piece of paper he could spot. Astonishingly, the paper converted into solid ground. He and Lester jumped onto it. Suddenly, it rose high up in the air, like a skyscraper.

'Whoa. What was all this?' Lester asked.

Alex explained everything to him, starting from the seventh challenge to the present moment. '...And I guess the more surface area it gets, the faster this badge does its work,' he ended.

Suddenly, time seem to have halted. No one was able to move, save Alex and Lester. Even the rushing water mixed with honey stopped flowing.

Vishwaroopaha's voice, echoing from the heavens and intercepted only by Alex and Lester, said, 'Wow, I really need to take a bow, boy. Hey, that rhymed! Anyway, you're extraordinary. I must say, you're just out of the world. Oh boy, you two surprised me, flattered me in fact. No one has got this far yet. There had been about a hundred attempts, but all of those hooligans got stuck or died at the sixth challenge. I love your tactics, Alex! You're amazing! Without any of my hints, you figured out how to use the badges. You are a true gem! Most importantly, you did this to save other human being, which no one did. You have a heart of gold. But beware, Demon Angelina won't wait for long. She's piling up her newly made servant alligators to get at the height where you are standing currently. I'm here to barge into your business and assign you a compulsory quest to stand a chance against her. You must find a way to get to the chopper up in the sky and...'

Alex looked up. Sure enough, there was a military chopper hovering in the sky. Lester's face looked tense, as if it would implode any moment.

Let's Wriggle Out!

Vishwaroopaha continued, '... climb up into it. There, you'll get a surprise. Fly a little further, away from where you are now. Then, get that surprise down on this island. You'll find a vast desert. That part of the desert is different from the earlier one, and poison ivy don't grow there. You will find Angelina's handbag at the end of the tenth challenge, at the Prime Lever. You'll have to use the handbag's supplies to pull the lever down. As you do so, everything would resume back to normal—Angelina would be back; the animals would turn back to humans. Remember: For this task, you'll have to head northwest. You'll also have to leave Lester here, on his own, and complete the quest yourself. It's time to test Lester's bravery. Hey, Lester, I hope you wouldn't mind thinking of a plan to prove yourself, and get Alex to the helicopter. Remember: Commands are to be followed. And, Lester, I have complete faith in you. You are a mastermind, boy, but you haven't explored your inner qualities yet. You must be prepared and have courage at all times. And, Alex, don't worry about Lester; he'll defend himself until you pull down the Prime Lever, won't you, Lester? After that, things will become normal. Your friends will find the way to you. Do remember, the surroundings are going to be deceptive, so don't rely only on your eyes and ears. Think of the consequences. Actually, there's more to the tenth and final challenge than meets the eye. It has a mini quest embedded within it. Wish you in advance, a...' he paused for a while, eventually ending with, 'Happy birthday!'

Alex was stunned once again.

'How did he know it's my birthday tomorrow...? Can't even imagine. How far can this guy go? Has he got any limitations? I wish I could... hmm. Forget it,' Alex went on thinking about a series of questions.

Snapping out from his thoughts, he said to himself, 'Nah, there's nothing I can do. Let's just go with the plan.'

Just as time resumed, everything got moving again.

He asked Lester, 'Did you hear him?'

'Yeah. I heard. I gotta stay here. Commands are to be followed,' said Lester, a little disappointed.

'By the way the chopper is still too high to reach, as the elevated ground where we're standing is still a little far away from it. I guess I know how you can get in there,' Lester pointed to the chopper above, which was hovering over their heads.

'I have a plan. We can make use of the badges.' Lester continued speaking as Alex heard him impatiently, 'Gimme the second badge, the one made of metal.' As Alex gave the badge to him, he said, 'Listen carefully... You are gonna toss the fourth badge on my head, where I will place my backpack to increase the surface area of the ground that will be created. As soon as you throw it on my head, the magic from the fourth badge would cause the soil to emerge, making it a solid ground covering all over me and gradually increase in height. You'll quickly jump on the ground created over my backpack to reach the height of the chopper. Here, I'm gonna make use of your second badge to dig a hole in the soil for fresh air to pass through, which will help me breath, as I will be submerged under the soil, after you have reached the height of the chopper. I will keep your badge till we meet again. And finally, when all this is gonna get over I'm gonna come over to do a badges handover.'

In an attempt to cheer Lester up and get him back to his usual carefree mood, Alex saluted him. 'By the way, you are quiet adept at rhyming *gonna*s and *over*s. Hey, hey... wait a minute. You mean to ask when this is gonna get over? That's quite a good puzzle.'

'It surely is. You cracked my code. But, for now, it's time to execute the plan!'

Alex was amazed at Lester's new avatar. It was difficult to believe that his namby-pamby and placid friend would show up with such courage. He knew that Lester's life was at stake, but there was no other option. 'Commands are to be followed,' Alex recollected Vishwaroopaha's warning.

Dawn was breaking. Alex applauded Lester, saying, 'What a plan, bro! You wanna say that I must toss the fourth badge on your head and climb on to get to the chopper, right? But this badge shows up only at the top of the ground it makes... I'll *not* let you stay that way, covered with mud while taking the badge with me.'

This made Lester serious. 'The ground piled up over me will act as my armour. I guess even crocodiles, which are being piled up by Angelina, will take a lot of time finding me. I hope they get away, disheartened by my shield. I'll be under cover and safe,' he said.

Alex pondered over Lester's plan in his mind.

Lester continued, 'Anyway, you've given me your second badge. I'll use it as a little shovel to scrape a bit of mud off my nose for some air. Believe me, I'll be alright. You can trust friends, can't you? After all, this is the only way to get up there in time.'

'Okay. As you say.' Alex was startled to find a drastic change in Lester's personality.

He tried doing what Lester had asked him to. But as soon as he reached the same height as the helicopter's, cold wind blew rapidly and his face hit one of the copter's glass windows.

He woke up inside the helicopter, finding himself in his father's lap.

'Oh, so dad was the surprise for me! Really, Vishwaroopaha *is* a word-trap maker.' Alex was glad to see his father, as well as Clinton and Eric, who had come to his rescue.

He got up quickly, still feeling a little dizzy. He then asked them to take the chopper down without wasting time, describing the present situation in minimal time and with minimum possible words, but not forgetting to tell them about Vishwaroopaha. 'So now, it's time to complete the quest.'

They got down, and as described by Vishwaroopaha, found themselves in a vast desert. The surface was burning under the scorching heat of the sun.

'So... how did you get to know we're here, and came to rescue us?' asked Alex.

Eric replied, 'Long story, boy. We landed on this island in an Army aircraft, searching for you, but encountered strange animals in the jungle. It wasn't easy to survive, but we didn't wish to abort or postpone our mission while looking for you guys. Yet, it wasn't possible to stay healthy and alive in the heat of the desert. Fortunately, we had summoned a chopper for later, so we switched over to it during the search. And... something else happened in between... Guess whom did we meet before getting into this chopper?' he then added excitedly after a pause, 'Your Uncle Edward! Isn't it astonishing? Umm... that's another long story, about his presence on this island... but, anyway, we need to find the handbag of Clinton's daughter first. Right?'

'Yeah. Let's focus on that,' replied Alex with a sigh. Then he announced, 'So now, all of us need to head northwest, as told by Vishwaroopaha.'

After wandering about in the desert for a while, an idea clicked within him. He said, 'Maybe he didn't mean us to go northwest. He told us to *head* northwest. I think heads has some relation to the two sides of a coin... We'll perhaps have to decide it by flipping a coin. North is heads. Maybe he indicated that we've to go either north or west.'

'Are you stupid?' his father asked him, surprised by his advice.

'Nah, dad. I understand his words. He always indicates clues in puzzles or substitutes. Please have faith in me. Let's give it a shot.'

'Okay. Let's try it out. So it's...heads!' said Eric after the toss.

'We don't have much time, Alex. If this idea of flipping a coin turns out to be wrong, you know what'll happen. This is a *life-and-death* situation.'

'Okay, dad.' Alex took a huge gulp of air.

And so they headed north. Soon, they found themselves at the entrance of an ancient stone ruins.

Time halted for the second time. The wind stopped blowing.

'This time, Vishwaroopaha's voice was audible to everyone,' Alex formed this line as a part of his screenplay. It turned out to be right.

Vishwaroopaha said, 'So now, each one of you must brace yourself. This is the final phase. Remember, your quest starts in the extraordinary maze, created to check your brilliance and sharp-mindedness.'

He continued, 'Once you get inside the maze, remember to get out of it only at the exit where you find a pillar bearing the particular symbol you're going to see right now. Beware, there are traps to misguide you. Your job is to find the symbol and move towards the exit, while preventing yourself from getting trapped. However, identifying a trap is not easy. No matter how much they try to lure you, move out only through the correct exit. They are traps, remember, most of the time. So, good luck.' As he ended, a strange symbol appeared in the air:

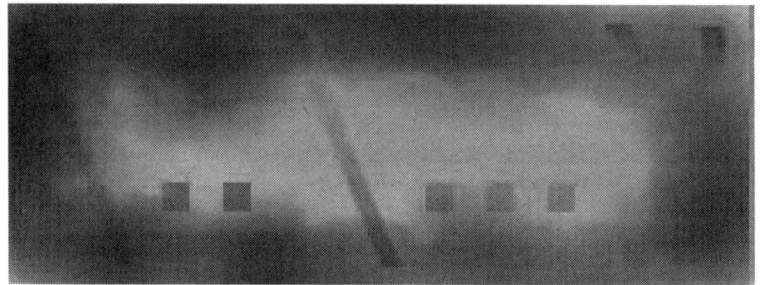

And then, time resumed.

'Was that Vishwaroopaha?' Alex's dad asked.

'Yeah, He is a quite deep man. But now, let's go,' said Alex.

Let's Wriggle Out!

He headed inside, with the dads following him. It didn't appear like a normal maze. It was a labyrinth of dark, ruined stone hallways. As they moved further in, they found a straight passageway, which showed up as the main path, with exits on both sides. At this point, the exits were few and far between. Walking cautiously, they looked around for the symbol. Alex realized that as soon as he entered the maze, the hexagonal split-image eyesight effect had totally worn off.

'One has to look for that particular symbol inscribed on the pillar and then exit to face his fate further on this island,' Alex said as he entered the maze and scanned his surroundings.

They kept on moving. After a few minutes, Alex turned right and found a pillar, with a dark mini-passageway adjacent to it. The pillar was giant, cylindrical in shape and beautifully carved with designs of ancient Asian deities. There were several other similar pillars that stood near each passageway.

They walked for an hour, after which Alex stopped at a particular spot, concentrating on the surroundings. He noticed something, and soon a smile of triumph spread on his face.

He called out loud to everyone, 'Hey, the symbol's here!'

'This challenge might've expected us to tire ourselves by searching further. What a trick has been employed in this challenge, planting a way out at the easily accessible place! What deception...making us toil for something already available at first,' he said as everyone came near him. 'But I've found where we need to go. See, here is the symbol and this is the exit.'

'That's... amazing,' exclaimed Clinton and they followed Alex towards the side passageway.

The four of them headed into the dark mini-passageway made up of stone ruins. It looked creepy and haunted, but Alex knew that it wasn't. After being on the move for a long time, they were exhausted. Their path had led them to the same main passageway.

'What's this? Where are we, Alex?' asked Eric.

'Alex, we had gone through the exit, didn't we?' questioned his dad.

'Did you identify the symbol properly or was it a mistake?' asked Angelina's dad.

'I think this is the trap,' said Alex.

Let's Wriggle Out!

'You have made a mistake in looking for the symbol, I suppose,' said his dad, with a hint of gloom in his voice.

While everyone had his own assertions, Alex, too, was in a state of despair.

How could he be such a fool? How could he forget that tasks were getting harder? How could he forget that the surroundings were deceptive and there lay traps?

They were fooled by Vishwaroopaha. The right place was not to be found so easily.

They continued moving on the main passageway, which kept narrowing as they walked further. They found a giant pillar similar to the one Alex had seen. All of them saw the symbol depicted on it. They looked at each other with joy, except Alex, who was a little doubtful this time. They went inside the mini-passageway adjacent to the pillar. Again they kept on moving in the dark, in a direction where the path took them. Though worn out, they kept on walking, keeping their fingers crossed this time.

After a lapse of time, they again found themselves on the main passageway, further tapering from both the sides. Disheartened and discouraged, Alex stood in despair, speechless now.

But he broke the silence after a while, 'We can't lose hope. There has to be some way out from here. Please have courage and let me think.'

'I have to look for some clue. Vishwaroopaha has never lied in any of the earlier tasks. Then how could he do so now? Symbol? Traps? Uhh... so many things to be taken care of...' he thought.

'We shall move again, but this time we'll examine the symbol for its genuineness,' he added.

'But how?' Clinton asked.

'We'll observe and investigate. That's what provides the clue to the next step.'

Everyone nodded and followed Alex reluctantly.

After moving through many trap passageways, Alex walked towards one of the pillars and touched the symbol, trying to understand what was so special about it.

'Why *this* symbol?' he wondered.

As he touched the symbol, a green-coloured magical hologram became visible, which appeared realistic, just in front of the mini-passageway adjacent to the pillar. It showed Angelina shouldering her handbag.

At first, Alex was scared of the hologram's sudden appearance. Unusual thoughts revolving around evil

Let's Wriggle Out!

spirits invaded his brain. But he understood that the clue lay in touching the symbol. Holograms appeared, blocking the passageway. The only way to get in the passageway was through the place depicted in the hologram, analysing the situation as shown in the display of the hologram.

All four of them touched the pillars' symbols at the same time, while standing at different exits, and waited for the holograms to appear. Nothing happened. No clue was provided. They kept on moving and touched symbols on different pillars. Holograms appeared but none could understand their meaning.

There were several holograms that lured them. One of the holograms that Alex viewed showed him and his friends' family having supper. He couldn't quite recall the occasion, but it seemed to him that he had a good evening spending time with everyone. 'A fake hologram,' thought Alex.

Another was of Angelina's handbag, lying on a raised platform. That was where he was destined to go, but he didn't see any Prime Lever around the handbag. So he concluded that this was fake, too.

Alex had finally understood this challenge. These were the hologram traps. He knew from the beginning that this was not a normal maze. Now, he also realized that it was a maze of holograms disguised as traps.

From then on, Alex's mind started running fast like a computer, to ascertain the purpose and connection of symbols, traps and exits. But, adding to his misery, he found none.

They kept on marching further into the maze through the main passageway. Alex noticed Clinton. It appeared from his condition that his heart might've suffered a major breakdown. He looked weak and was panting heavily. He walked over to a hologram display exit, which showed Angelina lying dead amidst a pack of wolves, who were ready to pounce on her. He was getting trapped by the holograms, and believing them to be real he started crying loudly until Eric pulled him back.

'I know it's hard for you. She's fine. Something as horrid as that will never happen to her. It's alright... Please don't get carried away. Remember, don't believe everything you see. We've to check for the right pillar,' he said.

From then on, each one of them looked disheartened, unwilling to work out their next move.

Let's Wriggle Out!

'Will we *ever* get out of here?' Alex asked himself, hoping for a happy ending.

After a while, the holograms looked far genuine than the earlier ones. Alex saw Lester and Angelina in them. Smiling, they appeared alright, their wounds healed. Alex was drawn towards these holograms, though he didn't lose his mind and patience like Clinton. He reminded himself, 'Everything I see may not be true. That's what Vishwaroopaha had said.' He believed in himself and knew that he didn't want to be fooled by them.

Still, just to confirm his assessment, he tried out an interrogation process with his friends through the hologram.

He asked Angelina, referring to her habits, 'Hi, hope you are well now. If I mock you, looking at your present situation, what would you do?'

'I would ask you the reason for doing so,' she replied.

Alex had not expected such a response from her. Rather, she would've said that she would hit him, mocking him rebelliously as a friendly comeback. He then concluded that this was not the real Angelina.

'But hey, she might've changed; become more polite. She's more courageous now... Anyway, now lemme interrogate Lester,' he thought, turning towards 'Lester-in-colour-hologram'.

'Hi Lester. How are you doing? Tell me bro, if you're gonna head for a treasure hunt contest and there are two ways to go—left and right, which way would you go?'

'I'll go anyway. It depends up the circumstances and my mood.'

Alex knew that in such a situation Lester would've certainly said, 'Right is always right.' He immediately stormed off from there, knowing that the test was successful and he had understood the deception of the holograms.

'This is not real,' he concluded and decided to leave the fake hologram display.

Once again, he joined the rest of the gang to search the desired pillar. From then on, the exits were situated closer to each other, with only an inch of wall separating them. The pathway's width tapered, too. After walking a few steps, they heard Eric shouting. 'Uh... I am stuck. This passage has narrowed so much that I am unable to walk through it...'

Let's Wriggle Out!

Eric couldn't fit in the continuously tapering pathway, so he took a side pathway that was broader. The stone wall that separated Eric from the rest was in ruins and ran parallel to the main passageway, enabling Eric to remain in touch with the other three.

'Anyway, don't worry. You guys carry on. I can see a mini-passageway on the right. Gotta meet you all again when this route joins yours. Everything is a trap,' Eric said, walking beside them in his separate path.

Soon enough, Alex noticed that the symbol always appeared on the pillars with holograms, and not on random ones.

'There are so many of them. How will we know which one will lead us to the exit?' asked Clive.

'Man, I am fed up of watching these. They aren't leading us anywhere,' said Clinton, who was tired and frustrated.

'Find some way out. You know better about these challenges than us,' said Clinton, turning towards Alex, while indicating the word *challenges* with air quotes.

'Something has to be done for sure. I can't accept defeat this way. All of us would surely come out of it,' Alex said to himself, trying to boost his own diminished morale.

Alex asked them to have patience and restart their search. All of them were terribly exhausted and disappointed, yet they went back to the task at hand. Alex too had lost his vigour and concentration, but somehow managed to stay patient and observed the holograms minutely.

Then Alex touched another pillar that contained the symbol, and something caught his attention.

He stood awestruck for some time.

'I see it...' Alex started saying.

'What? We have seen these pillars for hours,' his speech was cut off abruptly by Clive.

'Dad, I mean... I saw another pillar *inside* the hologram,' completed Alex.

'What? Really?' said Clive

'But where?' asked Clinton.

'I just saw it. Look at it. There,' Alex pointed towards a particular hologram. 'So, this is the trap. At last, I got it.'

'Maybe we have to go through the hologram which has the pillar bearing the symbol *in* it. I guess, this is just a clue,' Alex added, finalizing everyone's decision.

Let's Wriggle Out!

The hologram displayed Angelina's handbag, which lay in a desert, near a pyramid topped with Wasor's sacred colour—green. The Prime Lever was fitted in the centre of the pyramid.

Going through the space of this hologram felt great to Alex. It was very different from going through the earlier ones. It seemed as if a cool breeze had moved past him. He zoomed to the exit in a jiffy. Soon, they were out.

'Out, out of the maze, yeah. Out of the challenge? Nope,' thought Alex.

'Where's Eric, and why isn't he with us?' asked a disturbed Clinton.

'Is he still inside the maze? asked Alex, apprehensive of what could have happened to him.

Alex's dad said, 'Relax. Eric is perfectly safe. You already know that he couldn't fit into the narrow pathway we were walking in and had taken a side pathway. Through the broken stone wall that separated him from us, I had a conversation with him just a few minutes back. He had said, "I've seen a hologram with the pillar inside and bearing the symbol. Its hologram picture is..." his speech had quivered as if he had seen something unwanted and horrific but he went on saying, "Lester and Angelina are about to be eaten by a pack of wolves in a rainforest. I am saving them with a fire-lit wooden trunk in my hand." He had added, "There is one pillar in the hologram near me, and one in yours. I hope we'll end up meeting at the same place."'

After hearing him, I had replied, 'The three of us shall get out of this maze to pull down the Prime Lever and then everything would be okay. Hopefully, Angelina shall turn back into herself. Until then, your goal is to steer clear away from her *and* save Lester at the same time. Have courage, you can do it. Goodbye, until we meet again.'

While getting away, he had spoken the last sentence with a heavy heart, "Let's hope for the best. When Eric gets back, I guess we shall meet near the chopper, which will take us back to Florida".'

Hearing this, Alex, along with Clinton, went speechless.

Clinton broke the silence, 'Uh-oh. So now I got it... Do you remember that *Vishwaarippa*. Okay...yeah, that's not the right pronunciation, I know. But let's just get to the point. That man had used the word *pillars* in his long speech. Till then we'd thought that he had misguided us, and in reality there is just one exit and *one pillar* bearing the symbol. But now as Eric has revealed, I suppose there are two exits, two pillars and two symbols.'

'Nope. Exits could be two, but the symbol has to be the same on all the pillars,' said Alex.

Clinton looked around and said, 'Eric is nowhere to be seen. I think he's at some other place. It could be that the hologram near him displayed a different scene.'

'Yeah, tough luck for Eric,' replied Alex's dad. 'His destiny didn't permit him to exit with us. Anyway, to get out of the maze he will have to find and get through the place of a hologram exit,' he concluded, adding 'provided he saves Lester and they both return unharmed.'

'I wish and pray the same. Hope all of them are safe,' said Clinton, apparently thinking of Angelina.

Alex tried to comfort them, 'Let's not lose hope. We'll wait for them. But, till then let's finish the task at hand first. After all, getting Angelina back depends on us. We need to pull down the Prime Lever as soon as possible.'

Alex, Clive and Clinton found themselves in the middle of the desert. Angelina's handbag lay on the hot sand, and beyond it was a large pyramid. The Prime Lever could be seen in the middle of the pyramid. Alex was amazed to see the lever. True to its name *Prime*, it really was quite large.

Covered with rust, the lever appeared to be quite heavy. 'Even if anyone manages to get there, he may not be able to pull it down. Perhaps, even heroes like Hercules would struggle. Unless...Angelina's handbag...' Alex thought.

He looked through the bag, and observed that there were multiple toy guns inside it, with sticky notes on each of them describing its special function. At the bottom of the bag, there lay another note that said—*Remember: Each one of these can be used just once.*

This note explained why the *coldy-guy* gun was missing from her bag, 'Maybe it had vanished after use...' he guessed.

He turned towards Clive and Clinton and explained the significance of the handbag's contents.

'Let's quickly go through each of these and find out their functions,' said Clive, signalling Alex to do the same with the toy guns.

Alex then read each function aloud. But, none of the toy guns appeared to be useful in the present circumstance. For instance, there was one for a large firecracker show, one for a ninja rope and another for producing flames. There were few really awkward ones, too, such as the one for extracting chlorophyll out of a plant.

'Find the useful stuff out of the junk, think fast, Alex,' he said to himself.

He knew he had to be extremely careful with his next step, as the destiny of the four of them was dependent on this final step.

After exercising his brain, tirelessly looking for answers, he found two guns that he thought could be of some use to them. The first one was to make oneself merge into the surroundings, using colour-specific camouflage to hide. Another one was to make any object twenty times smaller than its actual size. Alex contemplated that only this gun could be of use to them. But, as he read the note again, he was slightly puzzled.

The gun would make anything twenty times smaller only if the bullet was fired in the object's centre. If the shooter fails to do so, the toy gun will transform itself into an actual one. And as soon as it happens, the former toy gun will raise itself up in the air and hit the handler... Thereafter, it'll perform its assigned work of reducing the target object size evenly.

Alex stared at that little piece of black plastic, still trying to come to terms with its strange workings. He couldn't even calculate the probability of getting it right in this case. 'A large pyramid; need to fire in middle; this can't happen...' a random series of thoughts inhabited his mind, and he felt that there was simply no hope of succeeding.

He took the gun in his hands, examined it from every angle and then walked towards the pyramid, leaving Clive and Clinton far behind.

Let's Wriggle Out!

'Okay. So, that's it. No alternative left,' Alex took the decision in a minute's time. 'At least, the work will be done either ways, whether the target is shot in the centre or not,' he thought.

As he pointed the toy gun towards the giant pyramid, he saw a glimpse of Clive and Clinton running towards him, shouting, 'No!'

Soon, the bullet was in mid-air... Alex had already shot.

Alex had failed to shoot at the right place, and he knew that he was slowly moving towards his death. The bullet hit him in the core of his neck. He fell on the ground. It seemed as if someone were painfully detaching him from his body, and his vision was turning blurry.

A minute later, he found himself amidst high clouds, making him realize that he was in heaven. It was quite cold. Just as he took a step forward, the clouds gave way, and he fell down. He couldn't understand where he was falling. He couldn't know whether it was actually him or just his soul. While in mid-air, he saw thick dark green beams of light emanating from a small hole, with one ray moving straight into his bleeding but now healing body, while the others headed towards the animals of the island to cure them and possibly turn them back to humans. In no time, his soul re-entered his body. He realized that he was returning... to Wasor... to his parents... to his friends... and most importantly, to life.

'How did this happen?' wondered Alex. It could only be the Prime Lever. Perhaps it was pulled by his dad or Clinton. 'The curse was lifted; everything became normal.' As his soul dived back to his body, pain took over him yet again. But surprisingly, it subsided soon, and he seemed to know how this came about. Just then, his vision turned green—*Wasor* green and then black.

He came back to his senses after what seemed like aeons. After a short while, he stood up to find that the size of the Prime Lever had been reduced and pulled down. The lever now stood in the middle of *now-6-metre-tall* pyramid. He glanced around and saw that Eric was back with Lester and Angelina, the latter appearing to be dizzy, but at least in her human form. Clive and Clinton were behind them, chatting and laughing.

Alex approached the lot and exclaimed, 'Hiya! I've just returned from heaven. Thanks dad and Mr.

Barrette for getting in the *save my life mission*, by pulling the Prime Lever in time,' he looked extremely happy to see his friends again. 'Thanks... Mr. Watson for saving my friends. Thanks everyone for being united and defiant. Without your help, none of us would have been alive today. As for now, let's talk less and get back home!' He added.

After he uttered these lines, the fourth badge appeared, accompanied by a flash of green light. It magically formed itself on Alex's shirt, taking the shape of a badge in seconds, glinting on the shirt as it formed, as everyone watched the strange process in amazement.

The badge seemed to be radiating faith, making Alex feel the same unusualness that he had experienced when he met Vishwaroopaha for the first time.

When all of them were busy observing Alex's 'Wasor Badge Collection', he heard a loud whirring sound, as if emanating from large blades. Clinton and Erick started shouting, waving their arms for the pilot's attention. A Chinook landed on the hot sand, and after everyone got in, it proceeded with the journey back to Florida.

Chapter 16

Reunion

As the helicopter landed, blowing dust off the helipad in all directions, Alex noticed the far flung landscape of his hometown. As he stepped on the ground, he felt as if a huge burden had been lifted off his shoulders. 'Whew-huh? Back home. Easy as a pie, yeah?' he thought.

By the time Alex reached home, it was 9:00 a.m. Everyone bid goodbye to Alex and his father, promising to meet at supper. Later, Alex checked his emails to assess the situation at work. Unknowingly, he fell asleep on the sofa while he was planning the outline of a brief article about his experience on the island.

At supper, experiences were exchanged amongst everyone in the lawn. A little later, the guard at the front gate called Alex on the intercom to inform him about a man who introduced himself as *Edward* and wanted to get in. Alex told the guard to let him in. Soon, a pearly white Ferrari, with Alex's uncle at the driver's seat, entered through the gate. Alex approached him along with the three men and greeted him. 'Uncle...why, it's been a long time. About... 10 years since we last met.'

'Yeah, Alex. Good to see y'all. Good to...' his voice trailed off, as he started walking towards the table loaded with food.

'He's still a foodie, Alex. Don't mind him,' Alex's dad whispered to him.

'Yup. I can see that. Notice how he's ferociously gobbling the stuff? Quite abnormal...'

'Hey boy, don't be suspicious. He's just... oh Jesus,' his dad said, rushing to Edward's aid, as he had suddenly started to vomit.

At night Alex lay in bed, intuitively thinking about Uncle Edward, trying to recapitulate everything. But, he could not find any link that connected the happenings at the island with his uncle.

Reunion

'Never mind, may be I am getting a little shaky, thinking of my own uncle as different. For now, I'm gonna have this precious bed all to myself. Sleeping on the ground was no laughing matter. Not a pleasant experience at all,' he thought, before falling asleep in his comfortable bed.

'Come on! Let's go! Get up, silly guy. You're gonna get me late for breakfast!' Alex woke up to see Uncle Edward looming over him. 'Hey man, stop it! You're nibbling my fingernails! I'm looking fresh, but that doesn't mean I'm a fresh apple or orange... I'm your uncle Edward, boy.' What Alex had thought of as his own thumb, turned out to be someone else's. He quickly withdrew it from his mouth.

He then sat up straight and looked at Uncle Edward. In the morning sunlight, Uncle Edward glistened like the divine. Combed hair, sparkling brown eyes and... okay, *there was* a large belly, but... he looked quite... nice.

'Yeah, uncle. I'm up. But...could you please keep your voice a bit down?' Alex replied, gearing up for the special day—his birthday—only to realize that uncle was already heading towards the dining room. 'Huh? His hobby is... eating? Nah. He eats like... No comments,' Alex smirked, as he reached the breakfast table after brushing his teeth. Uncle was still gobbling the stuff around him. 'Happy birthday, Alex. In for breakfast? Have a seat,' his mom wished him as he seated himself.

'Umm... no, mom. I'm not in the mood for breakfast today. I'd rather prefer a brunch in a mall,' Alex replied, scared of uncle's eating—rather #*Gobbling* habits.

'It's a weekend... There's gonna be a huge rush at the mall. Let's head to the golf club first!' he decided, and was quite excited to explore his city after the Wasor escapade.

'Fortunately, or... Unfortun–nope. Uhh... *whateverly*, uncle is tagging along with me. Still, no comments, right?' Alex smiled and said to Lester in his car, while they waited for Alex's uncle to show up, so they could all get going. He came up, at last, stuffing a chocolate-chip cookie in his mouth. '*Hi, boeesh. Letsh gho!*'

Alex drove them to the golf club. At the end of the day, he was quite... *happy*, and found Uncle Edward to be *really* humorous. It was a good experience to know him. With non-stop fun, he had a great day—

Reunion

spending time at the golf club, and later at the mall, after which they headed to pick Angelina up from the school farewell party for twelfth graders, and finally to the beach.

As they wished good night to each other, Uncle Edward placed his hand on Alex's shoulder and said, 'Remember me?' leaving Alex in a state of curiosity.

While in bed, Alex thought of this line from uncle. Of course, he remembered him. But he noticed that there was something different in his tone. It seemed Uncle Edward was trying to indicate that Alex needed to remember something else or, probably, someone else. For once, he recalled to have seen a tinge of sparkling lightning blue colour in uncle's brown eyes. He was startled.

When they were at Wasor, uncle had met Eric, Clinton and Clive too. 'There was indeed some connection…' Alex thought about it over and over again, sometimes sitting up straight, sometimes lolling over the bed. He even searched the web for 'Uncle Edward's Mystery', but realized he had gone too far, and decided to stop it. Yet, he couldn't get the thought out of his mind that uncle did appear quite different from earlier times. He never ate like a glutton, and was very sophisticated. His behaviour seemed extremely different from what it was ten years back. Unable to make out the cause, the absurd thought kept disturbing him through the night. He wasn't able to sleep a wink.

Then, at about midnight, something struck him, making him jump out of the bed. A terrible conclusive clue hovered inside his mind. 'With his signature brown eyes, uncle looked somewhat like... Vishwaroopaha,' this was the final line of his screenplay.

Suddenly, he heard a furious knock on the door. He let Uncle Edward in, surprised to find him there at that hour. He guessed that the weirdness that had followed them at Wasor hadn't ended after all.

Noticing Alex's suspicious expression, Uncle Edward spoke up. 'Yes boy, you're right. I'm him... the hard-luck sufferer. I just needed a better lifestyle, so I agreed to come here. Someone, rather, something sent me here. I could have never come here on my own. Don't mind me. I'm someone... just someone... just here to help you and help myself to some food. The *magic* has sent me to become a permanent part of your life. A man with a little bit of occult, that's it. By freeing the people of Wasor, you've got me, to help you throughout your life. At least that's my perception. You've already guessed who I am. By the way, let me not ruin your sleep. I could've said this at some other time, but I felt today was the most appropriate day. Goodnight Alex,' saying this, Vishwaroopaha headed out of Alex's room.

Just as he always did, he left Alex—***stunned***.